AH, FATHER

Mike Hales

Copyright © 2024 Tregonning Press

All rights reserved. Shift
ISBN:9798327464308

FOR MARGARET

Chapter one

Jennifer's whole body twitched visibly and involuntarily as if she were on a hospital resuscitation bed instead of a softly-padded sun lounger by the pool at the Beverly Hills Hotel. She hadn't heard that name in more than 15 years, and she turned, as slowly and as dispassionately as she could after such a shock, to see who had called it out.

Her poise was perfect. Right shoulder slightly raised, leaning on her left, her breasts straining inside a slightly less than conservative emerald green bikini, with the pressure of the swimsuit and the apprehension that had momentarily chilled her body.

Her composure swiftly regained, she affected the nonchalance of a stranger seeking to establish what had broken the peace of the moment. Subconsciously she lightly touched her expensively styled and coloured hair - subtle blends of blonde highlights in a playful cut that framed and complemented her distinctively beautiful face.

She knew that she could still stop a man at 100 paces if she were so inclined.

Her look, filtered by the deep grey of her prescription sunglasses concealing vivid blue eyes, focused on a young man, boyish even; not tall but possessed of a thick mop of hair and a self-assured grin - very much in the style of a young Jack Kennedy. He wore a white shirt and a lightweight beige suit with the jacket slung over his left shoulder. Very Kennedy, she thought.

Further detail was difficult to discern as he was approaching from the direction of the sun, a common tactic of the enemy she thought in passing. But why an enemy, she wondered?

Certainly the name had come confidently from his lips as he continued to approach her, slowing down imperceptibly as though a shadow of doubt had crossed his intent.

He said it again, purposefully, though only loud enough to remain discreet in the crowded pool area of California's most celebrated hotel " Pamela."

"Are you talking to me ?" said Jennifer in a pleasant enough tone, indicating a certain intrigue on her part that this not unattractive man should be seeking her out. He seemed quite at ease in the overtly wealthy environment.

The other groups of people nearby - slick, ageing lawyers, sharp-eyed entertainment types, each attended mostly by young, sculpted creatures with the occasional woman of maturity and style orchestrating the gathering - took little notice of the latest arrival. He was noted, catalogued and found to be missing from their mental lists of 'A' level people of influence in this village of status - Hollywood. One or two women, and men, flickered a passing interest in the insouciant young man.

Jeremy Leake was probably missing from lists 'B' to 'D' too. He had only latterly been a more regular visitor to Los Angeles since his emergence as a player in the music industry. Previously LA had never really been part of his playground, which stretched from the UK to southern Europe and westwards to the Indies.

So the strength of his purpose had not been seduced for a moment by the freeways, the warmth of the smog-filtered sun nor the villas of Beverly Hills and the vast billboards of Sunset Boulevard.

"Pamela," he said again, this time with some assurance that he had found his target. "You're a long way from home."

"I really don't know what you are talking about," said Jennifer with measured emphasis, now fully back under control. "Who is this Pamela person you are talking about?"

Jeremy had by now crouched near Jenny's lounger to bring his face more into line with hers. "I think you know what I mean" he said, his voice insistent but barely audible, especially with the murmuring buzz in the background.

"Perhaps we could go somewhere a little quieter and talk."

"I'm afraid that I'm not in the habit of just going off with a strange man to whom I have not even been introduced," said Jenifer with as much severity as she could muster. They may not have been introduced, and her statement was being a little economical with the truth, but this 'boy' seemed somehow attractive.

Jeremy stood up slowly. "Well, I don't know if these people want to hear my story, probably not. But, on the other hand, where better than Hollywood to turn this little plot into a blockbuster?"

Jennifer started to feel uneasy. This man clearly knew something about her, and she couldn't place him in the pantheon of faces from her earlier life. She tossed all manner of thoughts around her head in a matter of seconds as she desperately sought to regain her cool and stay on level terms with him, if not ahead of whatever this game was.

"Well, the sun is getting a little strong here, perhaps we could spend a few minutes in the Polo Lounge with a cooling drink, while we try and find out who this Pamela person is you're looking for," she responded with studied calm.

A crisp, ten-dollar bill to the captain at the pool had led Jeremy to the impressively tanned body in an emerald-green bikini, topped by blonde highlighted hair and a pair of expensively-framed grey sunglasses.

She was a cool, sophisticated woman, probably ten or 15 years older than he, but the more attractive for her casual charm underpinned by a steely experience. She was very attractive. He had clearly captured her attention at the pool - now for the kill.

"Good _morning_, Miss Hawes. How nice to see you today," Emilio the maitre d' of the Polo Lounge oozed surprisingly sincere charm: "Will you be joining us for a little light lunch ?"

Jennifer had draped herself in a diaphanous wrap more in the style of a sari than a sarong but certainly opaque enough to conform to the Polo Lounge dress code. "No thanks, Emilio, I just need to cool down a little from the sun. A table inside please and a freshly-squeezed orange juice. What will you have..?" she let the question hang since she still did not know this man's name.

"The same for me," said Jeremy as Emilio swept them with a flourish to a corner booth in the shady bar. He whisked away Jeremy's jacket.

Jennifer was back on top and in her element in this most cosmopolitan of bars. Almost every other person checking with Emilio at the desk was a star of some magnitude from screen, stage or the music charts. She felt strong in dealing with this still cute young man, but she retained her dark glasses, partly for the effect, partly to disguise the anxiety in her face and partly so that she could see sufficient detail to move around at all. Best get his story out of the way before she might arrange a little action, she mused to herself.

"So. Let's drop the pleasantries. Who are you and what do you want?" said Jennifer briskly and with an air of finality.

"My name is Jeremy. I work in the music business, look after a few artists and generally fix things up for them. I have, er, a friend, who is trying to sort out a problem and I have agreed to see if I can fix it for him.

"I know people in the weirdest places for some quite obscure reasons, and when I started talking around trying to find a solution to my friend's problem, your name cropped up - at least, _one_ of your names."

"Wh-e-ll," said Jenny with a theatrical emphasis, "that's one of the more original chat-up lines."

She studied the young man sitting across the alcove from her on the effortlessly comfortable green banquettes. He must be in his thirties - but only just - she decided and cast her eyes over his slim frame, crisp white shirt thrice unbuttoned, and his beige suit trousers pleated in the front and snug round his rather perky little bottom. Hmmm, this is an interesting one.

As she half-listened to him, Jennifer's mind started to range back over her past life trying to find a connection with this Jeremy which might give her a clue about him. But for the time being she was just enjoying the view and imagining the prospects unfolding in the Polo Lounge - hub of social intercourse among the glitterati created and nurtured in this fantasy land called Hollywood.

As she later told her bosom buddy, Melanie, on the phone from her mini-suite at the hotel "if one is going to have a toy boy lover, he might as well be boy enough to toy with! "

Chapter two

The journey had begun badly for Jeremy, as travel seemed to do on his personal trips when he had to organise things for himself, without the cocoon of business-class used for his professional travel.

He had been impatient with the necessity of arriving at Heathrow more than two hours ahead of departure. He was irritated by the long queue of fellow-travellers, nouveaux-riche to a man, and patently lacking any sense of style or social grace with their cheap track-suit bottoms, ostentatiously branded trainers and synthetic England football shirts (and they were only the fat ones, he mused darkly). There they stood, cackling loudly about the minutiae of their unexceptional lives. And he was angry when deposited by the computer in a seat five rows from the back of the plane.

He hated the far end of any plane. How come he had arrived early, checked in ahead of many of these 'mongrels' and yet it would appear that more than 300 seats had already been booked on this poxy plane ?

No amount of heated argument with Miss Bland at the check-in counter could persuade her or her supervisor to move him to a forward aisle seat or, heaven forbid, upgrade him to business or first class. He would have tried his legendary charm with either sex but that had long since deserted him on this particular day.

Once in his seat on the plane, he fiddled gloomily and aggressively with the headset and controls and his mood darkened still further when he could only tune in one channel of blurred sounds of sixties pop, and the comedy channel was inaudible.

But barely an hour into the flight his mood lifted. Flight attendant 'Barbara' brushed against his arm once too often to be careless. Jeremy had dismissed the rest of the crew as unattractive, which had only served to deepen his gloom. Why, he wondered, did the airlines seem to major on women attendants with fuller, briskly married figures and clearly gay stewards. Not that either would have represented an appreciable handicap to him if he had been in the mood, he scowled to himself.

He hadn't noticed Barbara earlier and now she seemed to be ever-present around the rear seats, moving smoothly up and down the aircraft aisles and back to the kitchen area just behind Jeremy. He hatched a cunning plan.

Moving his glass of scotch and ginger ale (with extra ice) towards the edge of his tray wedged just above his knees, he eased his elbow out across the hard arm of the seat and waited.

Bingo ! Barbara cruised back towards the kitchen area just a shade too close to his arm and over went the drink, across his book and into his lap.

"Oh, I'm SO sorry!" she rushed with the ever-present smile. "Here, take these napkins and I'll go fetch a cloth. I'm SO sorry." Her voice trailed off ahead of her as she busied her way back to the kitchen, returning in moments with a cloth, which she handed to Jeremy. Shame, he thought, smiling inwardly as he attended to his rather damp lap.

"It's OK. Don't worry" said Jeremy with a broad grin. "My fault for being so wide."

"Let me get you another drink," said Barbara, trained to perfection. "No, that's fine, thank you," responded Jeremy. "I'll come and get one in a minute. I may need to pop into the bathroom to sort this out first."

After she had gone about her service, Jeremy allowed himself a small chuckling grin. The old touch had not deserted him. On to stage two.

Letting five minutes or so elapse he rose to his feet and extricated himself from the tight economy seat and moved steadily along the few feet of aisle which took him to the galley area where Barbara was waiting on more hot water for coffees.

"I should really chastise you for this." Jeremy spoke in a low, light voice and the accompanying grin on his boyish face conveyed exactly the message he wanted to get across.

Barbara said nothing. Her body language said nothing but professional flight attendant. She picked up the coffee pot and just shot him a look as she turned her back and headed out into the opposite aisle.

As her powder blue skirt and white patterned shirt moved up the aisle turning first this way and then that with offers of coffee, Jeremy stayed rooted to the spot, his confidence dented if not draining steadily away. Was she really going to blank him, or was there just a glint of fire in those eyes as she turned away?

For perhaps the first time in his life Jeremy wasn't sure. So he waited.

Barbara returned to the galley, her coffee pot empty once more. "Look," she intoned quietly but firmly, "come back in 20 minutes when things quieten down, and we can talk about it."

So she had got the message but she was being cleverly ambiguous in her reaction. Was she receiving the message or was she just preparing the way for a firm rebuff straight from the flight attendant manual ?

Jeremy ambled the few steps back to his seat. His mind was full of Barbara.

What was going to happen ? Would this cool beauty, easily the pick of the cabin crew, play along with his flirtatious suggestion ? He let his mind wander over her tall, elegant appearance, her apparently natural blonde hair pulled into a knot clamped with a tortoiseshell clip, and her enticingly-shaped legs, slim with well-defined calf muscles - the best.

He caught her eye as she moved once again along the further aisle and this time there was just the flicker of a smile before she turned to the next passenger with her tray of extra milk and sugar.

Jeremy grabbed his book and looked at his watch. Still 15 minutes to go. On roared the plane, stable and seemingly anonymous in the sky.

From time to time he watched the team of attendants moving constantly around the cabin full of West Coast travellers. Gradually the momentum eased and the assembly turned its attention to the first movie. Window blinds went down and the pictures started to flicker onto the various screens about the cabin. The usual few stubborn readers pressed their individual spotlights into action but the space settled into a Hollywood viewing theatre in the sky. It was time.

Jeremy once again eased his slight frame through the necessary contortions to free himself from the seat and turned towards the galley.

A couple of flight attendants were already sitting in quiet, animated conversation - probably about schools in Esher, thought Jeremy brightly. One of the camp icons darted off towards the centre service area where presumably his friend was stationed, and then there was Barbara, standing purposefully tidying the galley area and clipping shut the metal containers.

She turned towards Jeremy without surprise and started moving past him. In one continuous motion she brushed alongside him, caught his shirt between finger and thumb and hissed "I'm going to the bathroom" as she moved out of the galley, out of sight of her colleagues and behind the heavily-engaged heads of the passengers, into an empty toilet cubicle......................

It was brilliant sex. Not the leisurely, languid Sunday morning sex, nor even the intense Saturday night variety after perhaps one too many drinks. This was urgent, brutal, necessary sex and absolutely of the moment. Barbara half-gasped, half-sighed as Jeremy climaxed within a few minutes.

Not her first visit to the Mile High Club, thought Jeremy as he set about recovering himself. Wow, what a tornado ! It's barely 2pm London time and scarcely more than 6am in Los Angeles - what a start to the day !

"Complimentary book of matches, sir ?" said the stewardess as Jeremy eased his way towards the door of the 747 at Los Angeles airport. He looked up straight into Barbara's practised, professional smile alongside her colleagues bidding farewell to the motley collection of passengers. He could hardly miss the coquettish raised eyebrow as she dropped the matches into the top pocket of his jacket.

'Well,' he thought ' this is going to be an interesting trip' as he steered the rented flame red Thunderbird towards the freeway and ultimately Sunset Boulevard and the Beverly Hills Hotel.

Jeremy had not previously stayed at the legendary Beverly Hills Hotel. He was more of a Chateau Marmont guy down on the Strip, where the rockier element of rising stars of music and film tended to stay.

The Beverly Hills was more for the upper echelons of the entertainment industry, behind and before the cameras and very much behind the hit-making machinery of the music business.

Nevertheless he had a hunch that was where his quarry would be staying, so he had pooled his credit with his brother and made a reservation, managing to combine the trip with some music business to offset the cost.

Once in his large and impressive room - super king-size bed and space still for a small sofa, coffee table and chairs - Jeremy retrieved the matches from his jacket. 'Call me - Marriott - Barbara Andrews xx', it said inside the British Airways flap.

So he did, but first he had to be sure that his trip would yield a result of some sort other than the usual fun and frolics of musicians, groupies and record company middle management out to impress their British cousin – not to mention the odd pick-up on a plane.

He had confirmed at the front desk that Jennifer Hawes was staying in the hotel and he left a note for her in the hotel's embossed envelope. Jeremy showered, hung up his set of fashionable clothes and selected a Paul Smith suit with a faint purple hue and a soft pink button-down shirt to go with his rich tan boots.

It had been a long flight and the combination of the massaging shower and the adrenaline rising at the evening in prospect kept Jeremy's fatigue at bay. Miss Hawes might ring at any time, but patiently waiting was not high among Jeremy's attributes so she would have to wait until he was ready.

He spent the rest of the afternoon making calls and catching up on American television with its weird palette of colours featuring mostly orange, red and green. One day they'll get a decent system, thought Jeremy. By seven he was ready for a little action.

The living is easy at the Beverly Hills Hotel. That's the way it's designed to be. As you pass through the front doors in the lobby, the valet parking attendant is climbing into your car somewhere deep in the garage to bring it to the end of the canopy in the driveway by the time you have walked the twenty yards or so of carpet. Sometimes they miss by a matter of seconds but it's still impressive - even to someone already as jaded as Jeremy.

He walked around the Thunderbird, remembered the ten-dollar tip for the captain holding open the door, and folded himself enthusiastically into the driver's seat. He laughed inwardly as the great beast growled round the drive and eased powerfully to a halt at the street - Sunset Boulevard, street of legend and the very essence of Hollywood in its broadest sense, since the hotel stands squarely in the midst of opulent Beverly Hills. They work in Hollywood but they live in Beverly Hills, he thought.

A sharp hoot on the horn from the car behind brought Jeremy back to some sort of reality as he ran over the possibilities afforded by a hot stewardess. For now he was out to play with Barbara Andrews, the mile-high clubber, and Jeremy was very good at playing.

In fact, it had largely been his career for the past ten years or so. His easy charm and his nonchalance had given him entree to many a party salon, night-club, yacht, mansion, apartments and the beds of hedonists - male and female.

His contact book in itself was the stuff of potential legend and he was beginning to exploit its flexibility to further enrich his progress through life. But first he had this rather entertaining problem to sort out.

He pressed the 'go' pedal and turned the powerful Thunderbird east along Sunset Boulevard. He started to sing with the radio ' I Heard It Through the Grapevine.' Ola California !

Chapter three

Pamela Gerber had risen out of her soulless East Midlands home town. Cranby was the site of ten thousand little boxes built in the 1930s which, ironically, were maturing into respectable semis with larger-than-average gardens in green and tidy estates, with culs de sac and cut-throughs and more economy cars than had been anticipated.

The town centre - a collection of downmarket stores and small supermarkets amid council offices, a police station and the ever-active bookmakers - was a classic of post-war planning; grubby paved areas with litter-strewn flower beds stained with gum, beer and cigarette ends as the population lingered in hope and frustration.

Swirling winds made it icy in winter and dusty in what passed for summer amid the all-pervasive grimness of Cranby's seasons. Even on the calmest days wind swept the town centre to topple the most recent hairstyle to emerge from the Shear Delight salon on the corner near a stone structure that used to be a fountain.

Most of the lingering was done by teenagers, cheaply overdressed as one, trailing hair, beads, cigarettes, crude make-up, bangles, skin-tight jeans, scuffed shoes and defiance all around them, as they imposed their presence on the sub-teens, who were relegated to the outer corners of the market-place, and glared a subliminally subservient threat to those older than themselves.

Loitering in the town centre was not for the young Pamela. Instinctively she had placed herself in the camp of the creators in society - those who looked for something new, maybe better; who pushed the margins of experience; who dared rather than endured; who participated rather than spectated.

She scorned the vacuous existence of the bored ones. Somehow she felt that life was more about experiment and novelty than humdrum and indifference.

Even as a teenager Pamela wanted to make herself open to new experience. She and her friends lingered in their bedrooms, talking trash about older boys and wondering what might be, how it might happen and what it would be like.

It wasn't long before Pamela engineered the first encounter and was able to report back on being held feverishly against the skinny, firm body of a boy as his tongue darted across her mouth in a clumsy but promising kiss.

Boys seemed to have no notion of connecting to a girl's sensitivities, she declared, beyond rather savage kissing and determined but misguided fumbling about the breasts, and groping outside clothing in impenetrable ignorance of the fastenings of women's clothing.

And thus it was with an air of profound disappointment that Pamela crossed the Rubicund of virginity in a tawdry encounter in the woods beyond Cranby. It was brief and clumsy, leaving Pamela gratified on the one hand that she had made the transition from girl to woman but deeply saddened on the other that there was no accompanying revelation of bold, new feelings and emancipation.

The boy was of no consequence. He, no doubt, would be regaling his friends with embroidered tales of his conquest whilst she told hers only of failed promise, discomfort and disappointment.

But from such inauspicious beginnings a life built around social intercourse in its broadest sense was shaping up for Pamela. Her appetite for control of her contributions to social activity had merely been whetted.

She could speak to no-one outside her small circle of girl friends. Her big brother was six years older and already a committed member of the footballing fraternity at the local working men's club and a lark in the darker reaches of the local flea-pit, laughingly called a cinema. He merely acknowledged her in his more amiable moods, which were rare enough in his busy but restricted outlook.

Her father, a graduate of the same football and men's club academy and now a pundit among equals at the matches, was a mild counterbalance to her mother's waspish temper when it suited him. But he was as immune to the complexities of a woman's temperament and thought pattern as he had always been throughout a predictable life of toil, beer, domestic submission and fraternal bravado. He was benignly inaccessible to a thrusting teenage girl and her contrary moods.

Pamela's mother had kept her slender figure and a pride in a tidy home in one of the semis, decent food on the table and an ever-present aspiration to a slightly more stylish and qualitative existence. She had provided the finance from her iron-fisted management of the household budget, and the pressure on her husband, to run an older but more up-range car than the average on their street.

And what she lacked in real sophistication and social vision she made up for, with her daughter, in an ability to listen, question and provoke debate on the tightly-focused needs of an emerging young woman. She knew instinctively that she could control less and less, but could still influence to a degree the more impulsive ideas of a daughter of whom she was maternally proud, no matter what, and whom she privately and increasingly admired for her obvious determination to move beyond the narrow frontiers of Cranby.

Few got close to Pamela and eventually she was generally ignored by the football/men's club crowd of apprentices and layabouts. Pamela's ambition lay in other directions, in places with which Cranby could not compete - or so she thought.

Her evolution from girl to woman was steady rather than swift, yet remorseless in its change from gangling girl to young woman with potential.

Then there was the question of what to do with her life. What seems to be one of the more profound decisions a person can make in their formative years often boils down to fairly simple lists of 'likes' and 'dislike.'

Pamela bristled like any self-respecting teenager at efforts by her parents, notably her mother, to raise the subject of post-school existence or, heaven forbid, a career. But in the cocoon of her bedroom she began to give the subject an increasing amount of time.

She had a natural exuberance for life and had already joined a gym with a swimming pool in the town to keep herself fit.

She knew that she enjoyed being amongst people and could comfortably hold up her end of a conversation in an interesting and engaging way. She didn't much care for routine or being told what to do and when to do it, preferring to scan the bigger picture for herself and plot a pathway through it in her own time.

But Pamela also realised that she needed to develop a skills set to enable the realisation of her preferences. Nobody was going to offer her a job for being nice.

So, to her mother's delight, she enrolled in a secretarial course to at least add shorthand and typing to her natural talents. There was certainly no intention on Pamela's part to become the personal assistant to any old boss figure. She wanted personal skills and some weaponry to organise her professional life, wherever that might be.

For someone with her intelligence the acquisition of 100 words a minute of Pitman's shorthand and 60 words a minute typing speed was a mere formality and achieved in less time than average.

Still uncertain of a way forward, Pamela knew that she had to start contributing to the household income so she responded to a small ad in the local paper seeking waitresses for a catering agency.

The work was quite regular and varied between occasional shifts in restaurants to quite large social gatherings in the various venues in Cranby and district and Pamela soon began to enjoy the steady income.

Dress was strictly black and if a shirt or blouse was to be worn it should be plain white. Pamela's nose wrinkled at the thought of such a uniform, but it was £2 an hour plus tips.

She had reckoned without the almost universal attraction for men of women, waiting at table dressed in black with a white shirt unbuttoned - with or without a small white apron.

At first the attention of sweaty, alcohol-fuelled fat men surreptitiously groping her bottom or sliding a hand up the rear of her thigh as she busied about their tables fully disgusted Pamela and she tended to react.

Eventually an older waitress took her to one side and gently explained a different picture, a more submissive approach that avoided the scenes and helped Pamela to dodge some of the more overt approaches.

She learnt too, that a smiling disapproval discreetly conveyed was generally accepted with reasonable grace as part of the game, and rarely did the perpetrator further overstep the mark. Rather, more often than not, he would quietly seek her out and press maybe two hours worth of pay into her hand.

Soon Pamela's tips were outstripping her little pay packet and she worked harder at the tease, safe in the numbers of her colleagues and the ultimate safety net of the often-present wife if the attention proved troublesome.

So Pamela became a profit centre in her own right for the first time in her life. She took care to give a regular sum each week to her mother to prevent further enquiry as to the totality of her earnings.

But her mother was no fool and certainly noticed the increasingly smart clothes that Pamela bought for herself. She said nothing but secretly admired. This girl had an instinctive sense of style - smart but sexy, quality mixed with bargain to create a look that became her own and began to separate her from her friends who were content to remain slaves to the brands of the teen mags and thrift shops.

Pamela enjoyed the cut and thrust of waiting at tables. It was tiring, exhausting at times, but the colourful snippets of conversation made a collective impression on her and she gradually developed a feeling that she would like to find a way into business life that promised more than nine-to-five routine, or simply being a waitress.

Having formed such a thought, it is often the case that focus brings about an early opportunity.

The relatively-secretive Northampton Knights of Showbusiness were an assortment of businessmen, sportsmen and a very few entertainers with roots or homes in the county. Nevertheless this motley collection had one thing in common - money - and often surprising influence.

That they did good work for charity, providing useful support for handicapped children in the community - buses for trips to the seaside, entertainment in hospitals and funding for special treatment in cases of hardship - was beyond dispute.

Their annual dinner was one of the most-coveted tickets in the county, but far lower profile were the stag nights at which it was rumoured that rather more than strippers provided the interactive entertainment. The rumours didn't move far beyond a restricted circle of society activists. The senior police officers present with several executives of newspapers and broadcast news made sure of that.

It was one of the stag do's for which Pamela was booked. This one was called The Arabian Knights for which the assembly was required to arrive in full Arab dress from headwear to flowing robes.

Some taking on fuel in the bar had difficulty with finding a pocket to stash their 'wad' - credit cards were rarely used on these occasions - but optimistically forecast that the evening would be as much fun as an earlier one with a Scottish theme, kilts and all that that implied.

Pamela looked forward to the evening. It promised better than average tips and the waitress staff were allowed to leave after the meal and before the 'entertainment,' although a few used the occasion to stay around and increase their tips at the same time.

No such thought entered Pamela's head. While the money was very welcome she was savvy enough to believe that her future did not lie among the 'honourable' Knights of Northampton.

The evening moved at a cracking pace. Nearly 300 men were socialising at full tilt. The air burst with great bellows of laughter here, there and all over the room at frequent intervals as the smoked salmon salad was punctuated with desperately sordid jokes, each intended to out-smut the previous one.

This was men bonding, networking, but most of all having an outrageously good time. By and large they were, if anything, less attentive to the nether regions of the waitresses than usual, knowing as they did that something far more stimulating was about to be unleashed upon them.

Nevertheless Pamela became aware of one 'Arab' on one of her five tables watching her. As far as she could see he was in his forties, quite handsome, very sun-tanned and had taken the trouble to wear a gold rather than white robe, marking him out as a little different, possibly with royal pretensions, she thought.

As she cleared the main course, almost inevitably a lump of chicken breast with what had started out as 'al dente' vegetables but which, for some, were more like a vegetable stew and gravy, he made his move. Since she was starting at his place to work around the table, he lightly gripped her arm and said, quite without irony: "You're a very attractive young lady. What's your name ?"

Pamela was more comfortable than threatened with his manner, and responded calmly. "Ah, Pamela," he replied, "how would you like some more interesting work than this ? More involved, but better paid work."

Her pause indicated to him both interest and distance. "My wife and I run a busy PR agency and we're always looking for bright young ladies to look after the clients. What do you think?"

"I have to get this table cleared. Please excuse me" said Pamela instinctively, managing to hide her real interest in this proposition. What did he mean about 'bright young ladies?' Was it just another waitressing job or was it a 'proper' job ? He had mentioned his wife right from the off, so it should be OK.

When she returned to the table with the creme caramels and an offer of tea or coffee, she made sure that his was the last pot of dessert to hit the table. "Well?" he said.

"Well, maybe. I'd have to know a bit more about it - like the money." Pamela was not slow to make her point. "Why don't you give me a ring and we'll talk about it" was the smooth, confident reply. He discreetly pressed into her hand a small business card.

'Ray Barnes, Managing Director, Sullivan Interactive Networks.' Pamela pocketed the impressively thick, embossed card and thought no more about it.

Some days after the 'Arabian Knight,' Pamela extracted the card from the small pocket in her black work skirt prior to dropping the skirt off at the dry cleaners.

She sat and looked at the card for some time. What should she do? Somehow she didn't feel the need to confide in her mother. This was something she could do on her own, she acknowledged to herself. But what was it all about? Would she be all right?

Never one to rush headlong into anything, Pamela decided to sleep on it and think about it the next day. It was Friday the following day and she could extend her consideration of this interesting proposal through the weekend. Maybe she would talk to her closer friends about it.

Making the call to Ray Barnes proved more difficult than Pamela thought. She had several times sat down and studied the card and imagined that this was possibly her passport to a more sophisticated life. She had become excited as she fantasised that she was a smart, modern woman in control of her life - and successful !

She fingered it this way and that; looked again and again at the lettering, the address, the fax number and, finally, the hand-written number on the back.

She had not discussed it with her friends. Once again the instinct for Pamela had been to take this forward on her own.

She stared at the number again. What was the point of looking at it? She knew it by heart already. Pamela became quite irritated with herself. 'Why are you dithering about with this? It's only a job like the one you've got. Get on with it.!'

She stepped into a phone-box and dialled.

"Ray Barnes" came the almost instant reply, soft but urgent and business-like. "Oh Pamela, how are you?" The tone changed to one of great interest and control. "I'm so glad you've called. Why don't we all meet up, you, me and Sarah and talk about the job?"

Pamela was re-assured that the wife was to be involved straight away. She had already heard stories from her fellow waitresses about men who offered all sorts of exciting opportunities at dinner events but who were basically looking for a bit of action on the side. Still, said some of the girls, if they paid up, what's to lose ? Hardly the point, thought Pamela.

She was impressed, rather than re-assured, when Ray Barnes pulled up in his Mercedes at the Roxy cinema where they had arranged to meet in the town centre. Pamela felt rather conspicuous standing there for ten minutes or more but at least there were four or five other girls dotted about the pavement nearby waiting for their dates.

Pamela smiled inwardly because she was looking so much smarter than them in her figure-hugging black cashmere dress with a little roll neck. She had put on a small gold crucifix around her neck resting on the dress. She was happy too that, whatever it may seem, she knew she was not heading for a fumble in the back row of the Roxy with some kid boosted by beer and stinking of cigarettes.

It was the first time she had been able to get a good look at Ray Barnes - and the impression was very satisfactory. He had close-cropped almost golden hair layered across his head with a right parting - a bit like Adam Faith she thought. His shirt was crisp and blue, still looking well-pressed at the end of a day, obviously expensive and he had the obligatory gold bracelet round his left wrist where she also noted a thick gold wedding ring on his third finger. He certainly wasn't hiding anything.

Pamela clutched her little red jacket to her waist as she carefully manoeuvred her bottom into the large leather seat before demurely swinging her legs into the well of the front of the car. She'd watched the royals do that.

Ignoring the scathing looks of the still-waiting girls by the Roxy, she turned to

Ray and said sweetly: "Hello!"

He reached out and touched her arm lightly and smiled as he pushed the great car into Drive on the automatic box and steered the Mercedes out of the town centre and away from Cranby.

Pamela felt that somehow this was a significant and symbolic moment. She was being swept away from the tawdriness of Cranby and the Roxy, but to what ?

As the car left the lights of Cranby behind and headed on the smaller country roads towards Belsingham Castle, a few miles away, the conversation was light. Ray complimented her on her appearance and casually enquired if she had a steady boyfriend - which she didn't. He didn't seem interested in probing her background any further.

Pamela asked him what his company did - Sullivan Interactive Networks..

"Oh, we are a PR and promotion company. We organise events for our clients and look after their publicity. It's a mixture of corporate and personal really because we have some big companies working with us and we also represent models and performers of one sort or another."

Pamela thought to herself that that sounded rather exciting and became more interested. Could this be her chance to meet some glamorous people - models, photographers, show-business people with money and ambition ?

The Mercedes swept past Belsingham Castle and down the hill into Belsingham itself before turning into an almost hidden lane off the main road. Within a few hundred yards the car turned again into a gateway overhung by trees and lined with high hedges. A long, gravel drive led to a large circular space before an imposing but somehow discreet house. The frontage was not huge but the impression remained that this was a substantial property. It was a world away from the cul de sac in Cranby where Pamela's compact semi vied for position with more than a dozen others in the space she had just been driven up.

Ray steered Pamela through a spacious marble hall eloquently furnished with antique side tables and a gilt-framed oval mirror to one side, into a small library-style room with quite the largest television Pamela had ever seen in the corner.

Sarah Barnes rose slowly, smiling as she stretched out a beautifully manicured hand to greet Pamela. "Hi" she said lightly. "Welcome to our little home," she added with a slight chuckle and a brief gesture with her left hand.

Sarah was a study in elegance. She wore a loose-fitting dress, almost a shirt dress unbuttoned casually. It was ivory silk and fell from her shoulders into soft pleats. Pamela was impressed although it was difficult to determine the full impact of Sarah's figure, so subtle was the clearly expensive dress.

She was tall with carefully groomed platinum blonde hair piled luxuriantly over her ears and held with invisible grips and strategically-placed combs.

As if to tacitly resolve the point of her hidden figure, Ray moved swiftly behind his wife and clasped her round the waist, kissing her firmly on the neck below her ear. Sarah was slender inside the dress, her figure still firm as the forties beckoned.

Such was the informality that Pamela began to wonder just what this job was all about. This couple in their late thirties were acting quite intimately before her without a shred of self-consciousness, and yet this was supposed to be her job interview.

The point occurred to Ray, clearly, and he let go of his wife, motioned Pamela to a deep armchair and offered her a drink. Sarah resumed her position on the sofa adjacent to Pamela's chair.

Sarah began the conversation: "Pamela, the world of PR relies heavily on networking, forming alliances and engaging people consciously, and sometimes subliminally, in promoting the best interests of our clients.

"It's quite different from events like the Northampton Knights.

"A lot of our business is done through highlighting areas of interest which might chime with the agendas of media people or related businesses, bringing such people together in comfortable circumstances in order to facilitate positive coverage in print or broadcast media.

"We organise meetings, presentations, and some social get-togethers. Sometimes we find it works better at home informally - very informally," another husky chuckle.

Pamela still didn't get a picture of what part she played in all this. They hadn't once mentioned waitress work. "So what do you want me to do? Pour the drinks?"

"Well," said Ray, laughing at her naivety, "that certainly helps, but there's an awful lot more to it than that."

Sarah stepped in quickly to the conversation with Pamela. "Pouring the drinks is only part of the game. We want you to be more of a facilitator, making sure that people get enough to eat and drink at the gatherings and encouraging the shy ones to circulate and meet people. But not in a pushy way, rather subtly and behind the scenes, as it were.

"We find that this initial role is good training for a possible future career in public relations as a whole. It's excellent that you already have shorthand and typing because those are skills that will be useful for the rest of your life. But you will need to understand more about communications, about expressing your intentions in writing, clearly and to the best effect for the client.

"But there's time for all that after we see how you handle clients en masse at our little parties."

She moved on quickly. "By the way, we don't do any of that black skirt, white shirt stuff. I like our girls to look as good, if not better than the guests. If you feel good you will be good at looking after our guests. We will give you a long dress. How does that sound?"

"Well, it sounds great, but what do I earn?"

"We will pay you £100 a week to begin with, with a £50 bonus for each party,

And some of the guests can be very appreciative of good service, so the tips are extremely good if you work for them."

Pamela was dazzled. This was a fortune of money for a young woman setting out into the world. One of these parties a month and she could buy anything in the Leicester shops, never mind Cranby. She became excited at the prospect and eager to go along with the Barnes' plans.

Sarah sought to close the deal. Ray had done well this time. This girl was almost perfect. She was impressed by, even attracted to, this tall, elegant creature who was still manifestly young and yet had a sophistication belying her years. Not the finished article by a long way, but the little uncertainty and the girlish eagerness were very appealing.

"Why don't I show you the dresses? Come with me, while Ray watches the news on TV." There was a confidence in her voice, which struck Pamela as similar to the mistresses at school - firm and expecting no dissent.

Pamela could scarcely believe the softness of the carpet under her feet as she pressed along behind the silken sashay that was Sarah in motion.

They entered a huge bedroom, bigger than anything Pamela had ever seen, with a bed that seemed bigger than her own whole room at home. She couldn't help letting a breathless "Wow!" escape her lips. Sarah smiled at the naivete. There were mirrors everywhere. Wardrobes - with mirrored sliding doors - lined one wall. There was a mirror above the head of the bed, partially obscured by the rich red drapes climbing to a huge bow from the padded rest for at least eight pillows - Pamela couldn't count in her breathless sweep of the room.

It took her several minutes to notice the mirror on the ceiling above the bed.

"Now let's see," continued Sarah consciously not reacting to the awe clearly expressed on Pamela's face, " you're about a size 10 I should think." She pulled from one end of the wardrobe a long, sheer maroon silk gown, cut on the cross and stunning in its simplicity.

"Why don't we see how this one looks. Slip out of that lovely dress of yours and try it. You have very good taste, Pamela, that's a classy dress for a young girl."

Pamela felt awkward. She was not normally shy with her body but that was with her closest friends. This woman was powerful, sophisticated and looked as though she had done it all and still come back for more.

"Don't be shy, darling," whispered Sarah in that slightly throaty voice, "let me help you." She was standing very close to Pamela, slightly to one side but facing her. She leant over Pamela's shoulder to find the zip at the back of her dress.

Pamela drank in the expensive perfume and peach-smooth skin and was overwhelmed by this woman's presence.

"There we go," murmured Sarah as she drew the zip steadily down Pamela's back, letting her face brush the younger woman's neck for perhaps a shade longer than necessary.

Pamela had never been near the couturier shops from which this dress clearly originated. She stepped into it and trembled as she and Sarah pulled it up her body. It slid over her like a second skin and came to rest under and just covering her breasts. She had never dared to show so much cleavage but as she looked at herself in one of the many mirrors angled about her she was thrilled. She was a woman of substance.

Chapter four

Jennifer studied the young man before her as he spoke. His quick smile, strong, white teeth and casual confidence were attractive. She noticed that the waiters were relaxed with him. He's either staying here or been to the Polo Lounge before, or both, she thought. Her instincts had been honed over many years of social engagement and had rarely led her astray.

"So, who is this friend?" said Jennifer abstractedly, pushing her fingers through her expensively cut hair.

Jeremy's words were a blitz of detail, much of which passed her straight by, but some familiar names and places snagged on her memory, so much so that she realised quickly that he had something of interest to tell her because he knew so much………

"We've met before," said Jeremy confidently. " You used to be married to a guy in television, didn't you? And you had a party at a really nice house in Chiswick - Bedford Park or somewhere like it"

"My," said Jenny very guardedly, " that would have been many years ago. Bedford Village. You're not that old, surely?"

"But it's true, isn't it?" persisted Jeremy. " Everyone was in fancy dress and you were a mean-looking Cleopatra. There were quite a few celebs there, mostly from television, which is par for the course, I guess. I can't remember what your husband was, though."

"Strange that, Jeremy," she enunciated his name carefully as though turning it over in her mind, as indeed she was. Who the hell was this chap? "Martin was a French chef, so you might have mistaken him for staff. It was his little joke. He used to like his food - 'never knowingly underfed' was his mantra."

"Used to?"

"Yes, I'm afraid he died a few years ago, poor lamb. Heart attack in the production suite during one of his shows." (Why am I telling him all this, cursed Jennifer to herself. I'm filling in detail for him and finding out nothing in return).

"I'm sorry to hear…." started Jeremy only to be swiftly cut off by a now restored Jenny. "You must have been a very young man at this party. I must be honest and say that I don't remember you, although I think I should have."

Jeremy noted the playful innuendo but decided to play it straight. "If I recall," he said, "I was Oliver Twist - a bit ragged and grubby and looking for more."

Touche. The corners of Jenny's mouth eased as she picked up on the flirtatious response. Hmmmm, she thought, he's a clever one.

"Well, we're not getting very far, young Jeremy," she said archly, "and I have appointments this afternoon which will not wait."

Probably a succession of boutiques in Rodeo Drive, thought Jeremy impishly. He was right, as it happens. "Well, I met your husband a number of times after that party, when I was properly introduced to him and he was not in disguise. In fact he was very much out, if you get my meaning."

Jenny pretended not to pick up on the clear double entendre and she, too, played it straight - for the moment.

"Oh, Martin was always out at some do or other, mostly industry or networking. I got bored with the same old faces." She had successfully concealed the clenching of her stomach muscles at the word 'out.' There had been times when she had suspected that her gregarious Martin had been playing away, goodness knows he had plenty of opportunity and he was an energetic, attractive - and a powerful - man in show-business.

It had never been an issue to cloud her mind. After all, she had enough little dalliances to keep from him - but at least they were with the opposite sex, as she had assumed were his. Theirs was a dynamic coupling which a few little ripples here and there could not dismantle - wasn't it?

Jennifer was more unsettled than she cared to show. This conversation was uncomfortable and yet she couldn't let it go. This Jeremy had some links with her past and there was a suggestion of menace about the way the conversation was drifting. She needed time to sort this out in her mind, but she also needed to hear more - a lot more - from Jeremy.

"Look darling, I have to go. I have meetings and I'm hardly dressed for downtown Beverly Hills, now am I ?" she laughed lightly. " Where are you staying? Perhaps we could meet later, or tomorrow ?" By now her mind was wheeling slightly out of control, a condition that she had long discarded as unnecessary and unhelpful to her lifestyle as a woman of substance, travelling the world.

"I'm here at the Beverly Hills," said Jeremy. "Maybe we could have dinner later? That way we wouldn't be under such time pressure."

"I'm not sure, I don't have my diary with me," lied Jenny, obeying one of the many 'Rules' a girl has to live by. 'Don't immediately accept a dinner date unless it is at least three days ahead and never at a weekend. Don't appear available.' "Call me later."

She was pleased, as she stood up to take his hand in a light reference to etiquette, that she had regained control of the situation after such an upsetting revelation. What were these meetings between Martin and this young man? She dreaded even to press the thought.

Jeremy inclined his upper torso almost to the extent of a slight bow as Jennifer swept imperiously from the Polo Lounge, acknowledging Mario's entreaties to return as she turned towards reception. Jeremy took in all her splendid body had to offer under the diaphanous robe silhouetting her against the sunlight pouring into the lobby.

Chapter five

As he brought the Thunderbird to a halt outside Palms, the most exclusive restaurant in Los Angeles, Jeremy felt reassured that his 'training' in the good life had taught him that aspiring to be the best means being the best. When you move in the right circles and stay at the best hotels - as long as you're not picking up the tab every time - then mere detail like getting a table at the best restaurant in town is smoothed away for you.

He dropped the keys and another tip into the hand of the rather good-looking young man who smiled to park his car (probably a 'resting' actor, thought Jeremy; might be worth checking out on the way home) and strode into the restaurant to meet Miss Barbara Andrews.

His confident and anticipatory smile checked and then widened as he was guided to a good booth to the side, which contained Barbara Andrews - and her very attractive companion Miss Lorraine Berry.

A glass of champagne stood before each girl on the table as Barbara effected the introductions. Lorraine, another slender figure, smaller and in exquisite proportion alongside Barbara, had very dark hair bobbed expensively to lobe length. She had dark eyes, which almost literally sparkled as the two women giggled at their fortune in finding themselves in such a place.

It was one thing to attend the busy and wealthy on board a plane, but it was quite another for two Surrey girls to find themselves seated among them - and a couple of movie stars - in Los Angeles' swankiest diner.

Jeremy took all this in as he ordered himself a glass of champagne. Even as the thought crossed his mind, Barbara answered his unspoken question. "Lorraine's from First Class, so you probably didn't notice her on the flight, thank goodness !"

Gallantly, Jeremy dismissed her modesty and proclaimed himself delighted to be entertaining not one, but two such attractive ladies.

"Being in the same crew, we do lots of things together," said Lorraine confidently. "If there's no fun around we do each other, or if one gets lucky and the other is interested, we play as a team."

"You can never have too many beautiful girls," said Jeremy, almost snorting with disbelief at his situation.

Given that the rules of engagement were so clear, the atmosphere was high flirtation and great humour from the first moment of the dinner. Wine followed champagne, slow-roasted pork followed aromatic starters of wafer-thin veal and tuna with balsamic vinegar among the exquisite taste sensations, which lingered one on the other as the conversation sped through frequent laughter.

Jeremy's invitation to the girls to go back to the Polo Lounge for a nightcap became more a matter of protocol than a need to progress the evening, and the gaiety continued as he studiously steered the Thunderbird along the streets of Hollywood towards heaven - Beverly Hills Hotel style.

The staff at the hotel from door to Polo Lounge affected a charming discretion as though a gentleman going out to dinner should always return with two winsomely attractive women, all in a state of enhanced excitement. Hardly surprising, as they see such behaviour on a daily basis, often with different partners of different customers. That could be tricky at times.

The trio swept into the hotel lobby and turned right into the Polo Lounge. Barbara and Lorraine nudged and whispered excitedly to each other as they spotted one star after another mingling gracefully in the crowded bar.

Eventually, after some persistent tipping by Jeremy, they were ushered into a cosy semi-circular alcove and, once again Jeremy found himself stretching out on the dark green velour in a whirl of anticipation.

The girls stayed on champagne but he relaxed into his favourite after-dinner drink - armagnac, and pondered with delight for some seconds over the range offered by the waiter.

Eventually he lost patience with himself and opted to let the waiter bring "the best" and turned his attention once more to these two exciting and excitable women facing him. But not before he had taken care to quietly order champagne and snacks to be taken to his room.

There is a certain sense of timing to these occasions and Jeremy was well practised in the art of bringing a 'liaison dangereus' like this to a peak and then striking, and after 20 minutes or so of sipping liqueurs and swapping flirtatious comments, Jeremy made his move.

"Let's go to my room and play," he finally said quietly to Barbara and Lorraine, who rose as one, with their smiles being response enough.

"Put on some music, Jeremy dear," said Lorraine, already moving around sensuously and pushing Barbara playfully. Jeremy fiddled with the sound system linked with the television and eventually settled on an r'n'b station playing its 'midnight lurve sangs.' It was the perfect accompaniment.

Lorraine was as good as her word and immediately took Barbara in her arms as they locked into the easy rhythm of the music. There was a familiarity - an intimacy even - that Jeremy knew he could not interrupt between the two women as they began to groove to the music. He sat on the bed and watched.

Barbara and Lorraine danced together close, the heat almost palpably rising between them as song succeeded song on the radio in the background. For a few bars their hands rested on each other's hips as they sashayed around the lounge area of Jeremy's room. He had already shrewdly pushed the coffee table to one side.

'When in Hollywood……………' he mused to himself.

Chapter six

Tonight was the first party at Ray and Sarah Barnes house and Pamela was under instruction to arrive no later than 6.30p.m. to meet her fellow hostesses and to get dressed for the evening.

Sarah was very particular about every detail, especially how the girls were made up and she had told Pamela that a hairdresser and make-up artist would be in attendance. So <u>that</u> was how models were treated, thought Pamela as she stepped into a bath at home, anxious to be ready before the taxi ordered by Sarah arrived to pick her up at 6p.m.

The cab was punctual and the drive uneventful for the 20 minutes or so that it took to reach Belsingham, with the driver only speaking near the destination to observe that "they're having one of their 'do's' here tonight, then" somewhat rhetorically.

Pamela did not feel inclined to confirm or even acknowledge the driver's remark. Her mind was racing with all the detail that Sarah had told her at their previous meeting and anxiety that she should do well in her first engagement as a private hostess.

"Ah, Pamela," said Sarah as she spotted the slender girl in the hallway. Sarah was already looking magnificent in a long black gown, backless to a vee below her waist and tied lightly at the back of the neck from where two narrow panels tapered outwards to the waist, scarcely concealing her large, firm breasts. Her hair, inevitably, was swept up into a tightly-controlled confection from which individual strands curled provocatively downwards, just breaking the line of her forehead and neck.

She was made up to perfection and presented a hugely attractive figure - just the image she had sought to achieve. In contrast, and as instructed, Pamela had simply washed and brushed her hair and arrived without a trace of make-up.

Sarah took Pamela to one of the first-floor bedrooms, which had been converted, temporarily, into a hairdressing salon. There were already two other girls perched on the bed in their underwear waiting as Anthony, dark, slim and smiling encouragingly, moved energetically around a third girl whose hair had been teased, sprayed and folded into a style not dissimilar to the hostess. It would not take more than a determined shake and a touch of one hand for the mane of chestnut hair to fall over her narrow shoulders and down towards her breasts, contained for the moment in a seriously engineered pink bra beneath a white towel - perhaps the ultimate effect.

"While they're being done," said Sarah briskly, "let's find your dress and get you organised. Then you can return to make-up next door before getting your hair fixed. I want you ready by seven please." Sarah took Pamela to yet another bedroom where the wardrobe doors were open revealing a line of very similar gowns, all in dark colours and ranging from satin to silk and velvet. Their commonality was a tightly-cut figure-hugging style which accentuated the female form at every opportunity.

"Ah, here is yours. You were the size ten weren't you? " Pamela nodded and gazed in awe at the dress, which made the previous model she had tried on in Sarah's bedroom seem quite conservative. She wondered quite how she might keep it on, so cut away was it at waist, bust and hips. In fact, the maroon silk dress had no back at all save for the ultra-thin straps running from the side of the bust and criss-crossing to the sides of the waist at the back. Best not show a lack of sophistication, she thought.

Pamela stepped out of her white shirt and black trousers and hung them with her red jacket in the other side of the huge wardrobe. Then, clad in her white towel and the briefest of knickers, she went to the make-up bedroom where two make-up artists were ready to transform the girls into radiant hostesses.

Pamela sat next to another brunette. "Hi, I'm Giselle. Is this your first time ?" Pamela acknowledged that it was and admitted to a significant degree of nervousness.

"I've done waitressing but they seem to want rather more here. Still, the money's great."

"It gets better," said Giselle. "If the evening really takes off and everyone gets into it, we can pick up loads more."

"What do you mean?" queried Pamela, half guessing at the answer.

"Well, you know, if we help the guests to have a good time, if you know what I mean, they can be very generous with tips. The thing to do is just relax, smile and go with the flow. Nothing bad happens and you get to have a good time and make loads of money."

Pamela could feel the adrenaline rising - part apprehension at facing the relatively unknown, part-anticipation and part-excitement at being in such a situation - worlds away from dour Cranby just up the road.

As her own transformation was complete, Pamela joined seven other girls in a dazzling group in the vast living room downstairs. At seven o'clock precisely the chattering stopped and Sarah walked in with Ray a step or so behind. She smiled.

"Most of you have attended one of our parties before and know what to expect. You know I run them with absolute attention to detail and that includes the welfare of my hostesses. I repeat the basic rules of our events as far as the hostesses are concerned.

"Our guests are here to meet one another and to get to know one another. They may go on to share an experience or they may not. Whatever they do, you must smile, forever smile, and make their evening easy and enjoyable. No-one must be without a drink at any time. You must keep an eye on the big picture of what is happening so that you can suggest to people who seem withdrawn from the event where to go to find an interesting group.

"The ballroom through there is close to the bar and functions both as a dance area and a casino. That is where guests meet and mingle. This room tends to be for more intimate conversations and…er…activities. And bear in mind that guests can go anywhere in the house, apart from your dressing room. You must circulate constantly and join in the fun if encouraged or invited.

"Bear in mind that I am supervising at all times. You will each be paid in cash at the end of the evening. Now, have a glass of champagne and relax."

A thrill of expectation coursed through Pamela's body as she looked at the group of girls - all tall, slender, beautiful and hugely attractive in their gowns in dark, revealing shades of red, grey and black. The others looked excited too as they started animated conversations across cigarettes in twos and threes. Pamela turned to 'Giselle.' "Well, here we go, in for a penny….."

Chapter seven

Jeremy stood stiffly before his mother's tirade. Even at 17, he was still on the small side, his thick hair heading in various directions at once as usual. Beside him, also at attention, was his brother Michael, ten years younger, with quite different rather dark and curly hair, equally dishevelled. They looked like two upmarket urchins.

"I don't know which of you is responsible for this," said mother, "but I hold you responsible, Jeremy, as the elder. You will go to your room and wait for your father to deal with you when he gets home. Michael, take note, and go and play quietly in the garden."

In her hand she clutched the note she should not have found which simply read, in awkward capitals, 'YOU AR A BARSTED.'

Jeremy, the recipient, though he would never have told his mother, stomped off to his room angry for a moment at the injustice, but gradually indifferent in the knowledge that his father would not take the matter too seriously. He never did.

Michael, an altogether heavier set child than Jeremy, thrilled with his success at getting back at his bullying and irritating brother with the power of the pen, dashed off to the garden to consider the consequences. No doubt Jeremy would find a physical, painful and secret retaliation in due course.

The boys' mother Lucy looked at the note again and smiled to herself. She was slightly shocked at the force and use of the language and realised it had been written by Michael. Of the source of such colourful, if mis-spelt phraseology, she had no doubt. It was husband Sam, a lawyer of some standing in the music industry where forceful language was the norm rather than an exception.

Their home was a comfortable detached house on the outskirts of a Surrey town. Sam had rapidly built his legal career and had been particularly successful in the entertainment industry. There wasn't much happening in the industry that escaped the attention of Sam Leake. Most of the big players had encountered him at one time or another - either as clients or adversaries across the negotiating table. He numbered record companies, pop stars and actors and actresses on the way up among his glamorous client roster.

By the time his father returned home surprisingly early in the middle of the evening, Jeremy was deeply engrossed in building a model of a seaplane from a kit, an activity which immediately embroiled his father. "So you got caught again, eh?" Jeremy emitted a noise some way between a hum and grunt, which passed for assent.

"Why on earth didn't you destroy the evidence?" said his father gently, preoccupied with glueing on the tailplane. "Silly note anyway, silly language - was it Michael ?"

"I thought so," he added after Jeremy's sullen nodding. "Just take your lumps and come down for supper when you're called."

The disparity between the boys both intellectually and physically was becoming apparent. Jeremy, compact, physical, outgoing and sometimes even charming, contrasted with his younger sibling quite strongly. Michael was quieter, more at ease with his thoughts than those around him; a reader and writer who tended to speak, even at this young age, only once he had considered what to say. He had the nascent shape of a tall, dark, well-built man whereas Jeremy was quite the opposite.

Michael recalled such moments later in his life and on occasion wondered how it was possible for two such different chaps to be the off-spring of the same parents.

Life at home, however, was more than comfortable. The boys' father was a clever man, well-liked and respected in an industry noted for its sharks and charlatans, with an income accelerating through six figures a year.

He was still handsome in his forties with a natural ability to engage with people, so his career progressed quickly.

For Jeremy the minor public school became easier and more fun as he moved up the years. He was a popular character and naturally good at sport. Though smaller than his classmates he was a decent batsman and an agile wicket-keeper through to the school first eleven and an ideal scrum-half in the rugby teams.

Unlike his brother, Michael won a scholarship to the same school, easing the fee burden upon his parents. Michael suffered sport. Whilst he was a respectable medium-fast bowler for his house team when necessary, he preferred the smaller team pursuits of cross-country running in winter and tennis in the summer and he made the school team in running.

Nevertheless, in the greater scheme of things, it was not that important. While Jeremy caroused with his sporting chums, heroes all in the school's ethos, Michael joined the debating society and worked on the school plays.

Despite the best efforts of the school, which had a good academic achievement among its pupils, neither Leake brother went on to university. Jeremy, already an inveterate partygoer at 19, simply didn't have the academic inclination, and headed off to London to a record company. His father had arranged the job and supported the boy, enabling him to take a flat in fashionable South Kensington and purchase an MG TD on the wages of an office boy.

Following on, Michael surpassed his brother and passed a couple of 'A' levels without troubling the university entrance boards. Whilst English and writing had been strengths for him, he was uncertain what he wanted to do with his life for some time. The one certainty for him, however, was that that he did not want to follow what he perceived to be the regimented life of his father in the time-bound world of law.

He opted for journalism on a provincial paper and headed towards the Fourth Estate.

Chapter eight

Jennifer sat at the walnut writing desk in her hotel room and stared at the multiplicity of black buttons on the ivory-coloured telephone. He had not called her later, as directed, and that ruffled her sense of superiority. Nevertheless contact must be resumed with this young chap. He clearly had plenty to offer and it was not all information.

She knew perfectly well how to dial his room but, for once in her adult life, she felt hesitant and unsure how to play the next scene.

The detail with which he had briefly regaled her in the Polo Lounge, of events in her past life - and his links with it - were quite sufficient to confirm that this was a man who had the upper hand, and Jenny never much cared to be bested. And yet. he had a cockiness, charm even, that she found attractive.

Throughout her life Jenny had been led by instinct when it came to making friends or taking lovers. This had maintained a spontaneity to her life as a merry widow, rather after the action of a pinball machine. Occasionally she would have a burst of ricocheting between two or three intimate friends, often returning to the same one for several 'moments' before sliding back to her flipper instincts and firing off on a different, apparently random but often calculated path.

Eventually, of course, she would exit to left or right and drop back into the assembled circle of good friends who watched over her every move. These were the satellites who endlessly circled Jennifer's sun, sometimes drawn into the warmth of her lifestyle, sometimes pushed to the colder outer reaches as it suited her mood and requirements. But never a day passed without a conversation with Melanie.

Money had long since been a matter of little immediate concern to her. Her darling husband - the first and possibly the only genuine love of her life - had built a thriving television production business. After his death she eventually sold his majority share-holding to the other shareholders and directors for a considerable sum. And she had invested her own modest gains from the property in the East Midlands which she had eventually sold.

Having established a reasonable financial cushion Jennifer astutely listened to her financial advisers and invested with a flair that served only to increase her resources. The management of her affairs was never less than a necessary chore for her, but the frequent meetings and constant letters and phone calls would have rather bored her, had they not been so important.

She had much more fun investing a little here and a bit more there in the various business ventures of her friends when they needed a little 'seed' money. From a couple of television features to the odd classic sports car, she rarely put a foot wrong in terms of getting a return on her money and she enjoyed the action - especially if it involved a special man in her life.

Thus her diary - a constant companion with its bulging contacts section - was largely driven by a mixture of socialising with friends; talking to advisers; travelling to interesting places; but most of all availing herself of satisfaction in the pursuit of pleasure. A comfortable way to spend one's life, she thought, rarely dwelling on the twin tyrannies of substance and direction.

But nothing came between her and the real action - meeting, attracting, romancing and finally seducing a new lover. Jennifer wasn't much given to female lovers per se but if they happened to come with the package then, hell, why not ? Life is for living, preferably intensely and without pause - no point in sitting back and watching as it flies by.

Jennifer had remained true in this respect to her roots in miserable, mean-minded Cranby. She had used her instinct to lever a passage out of that Godforsaken place where the biggest event in many lives was buying a new three-piece suite on hire-purchase.

As she sat now gently fingering the buttons on the telephone, she recalled the naissance of her affinity with relative wealth. Whilst fresh out of school she had found a way to earn rather more than her peers, which in itself had led her into an even more lucrative existence.

She was still in her early twenties when she became aware of the power that an attractive woman can exert on men driven to success and wealth, who were looking to sample the earthier delights of life whilst maintaining a respectable profile in their community.

Jennifer smiled involuntarily as her mind ranged over those early years. They had been fun - the thrill of discovery and realisation; the honing of one's emotional talents - the amusement of creating little whirlpools of sexual chemistry.

Suddenly she sat upright in the chair in which she had been mentally cruising – little whirlpools of sexual chemistry - is this where Jeremy fitted or was she attaching more significance than required to this disturbing, mop-haired kid? Kid? He had to be well into his thirties.

There was only one way to find out, she realised, as she started to dial.......

Chapter nine

Sarah handed each girl in turn a flute of champagne - neither a sparkling, golden vintage, nor a pasty imitation. She and Ray had long since finessed the exact level of quality that suited their Northampton circle so that it impressed but did not overawe these aspiring bon viveurs.

She surveyed the girls in contrasting long, revealing evening gowns and allowed herself a breath rather than a sigh of satisfaction. Most were regulars to one degree or another at her functions and two, including Pamela, were newcomers.

She wondered, as she always did, how the new ones would react to the goings-on at the party. An atmosphere of wild exuberance could develop really quickly with some partygoers, but she and Ray never let anything or anyone get completely out of control. After all, the point was for people to make new contacts - and enjoy them.

Already the drive was crunching under the wheels of some elegant and upmarket motors - one or two even with a chauffeur - and the doorbell started to ring soon after eight o'clock, the appointed hour.

At first Pamela clung to her champagne glass without once sampling the contents, mindful of Sarah's warning to stay in control, but she quickly warmed to the friendly faces and the attention that she, as a new girl, attracted. Wives and girlfriends in particular homed in on her while their men drifted towards each other in small groups where individuals had met before or had already done business together.

She remembered to smile and responded freely to the many questions about her origins and ambitions. She remembered, too, to be modest rather than too extrovert - another lesson instilled in her by her mother who was never one to 'rise above her station'. And yet her mind was on another level even as she exchanged small talk with the women.

Her function was to facilitate and introduce but, she constantly reminded herself, her future was more firmly pitched at a career of substance in the burgeoning world of communications.

Her eyes roamed slowly round the room as it filled with more people, people whose common denominator was smartness rather than style, dressed-up more than naturally suited to the demands of such a social gathering. Some looked almost apprehensive and as defensive as nervous. Others, especially among the men, exhibited a brashness little short of hand-rubbing anticipation. They were out for a lot of fun in whatever shape it came and they didn't mind who knew it.

All were suited and booted, some in formal evening wear. They looked particularly attractive, thought Pamela. Somehow the silk lapels and frilly white shirt with neat black bow tie ironed out a lot of the potential faults of a man who might be carrying a little too much weight - especially if the cummerbund was doing its job !

She mused too, while the conversation eddied around her, how easily one registered attraction or reserve when just looking at people. What was it said ? That one first look sends ten thousand messages to the brain about the person in view? Remarkable, thought Pamela. But it was true. As she looked from one man to another she almost instantly noted positive or negative feelings about them.

One man in particular occupied her attention rather longer than the others. He was handsome in a neutral sort of a way, certainly not ugly, and he had an easy smile. But it was his bearing that attracted her. He was casual but confident, clearly listening to others and letting them speak before responding in a way which commanded their attention and respect. He was tall, which helped, with fair hair only slightly receding at the temples, and well cut. His dress suit looked expensively tailored yet lightly worn. She mentally dubbed him The Prince because that s how he struck her - a regal air.

The women were a different story. They ranged from stick thin trophy wives with detailed appearance and just the right thrust to their busts to attract attention, to what is usually defined in personal advertisements as 'curvy' i.e overweight and struggling to contain the body mass in a dress rather overwhelmed, due to inadequacies in size or suitability. Pamela noticed more than one woman who clearly felt that a dress designed for a slender look should do wonders for her ample figure.

Pamela felt a marked sense of positivity or negativity towards the various types of women, some of whom were beginning to work the room, visually at least. Again, one stood out more than others. She too, like The Prince, was tall and elegant although she was by no means the thinnest woman in the room. Somehow she had managed the package very well, filling a long black dress which flowed from the hips comfortably and displaying a cleavage with the merest hint of age lines between the breasts. She was still an imposing and attractive woman who stood out in this crowd, stylish, confident and potentially provocative. Pamela dubbed her The Bitch - not unkindly but almost respectfully.

To the rear of the Barnes' house was a large rectangular swimming pool and adjacent hot tub with room for six people - eight at a squeeze. The house took up two sides of the pool and on the third long side was a pool house with the paraphernalia of pool maintenance and some tables and chairs. Its door folded open to the pool so that it provided some shelter when necessary.

Light steam rose from the surface of the heated pool on this cooling late summer evening and gradually a number of the guests started to wander around the patio by the pool, ostensibly admiring the floodlit gardens beyond the end of the pool, but clearly surveying the situation as the champagne began to take hold.

Sarah and Ray moved seamlessly among their guests, effecting introductions here, patting an arm there, offering a flirtatious kiss both here and there. They were masters of their particular universe, encouraging a dip in the pool 'plenty of costumes in the pool house - if you want one.'

Pamela wandered from person to person, offering a drink or taking a tray of canapes around. It was by now well into the evening, around ten o'clock and the atmosphere was loosening up a good deal. She noticed that the guests, both men and women, tended to touch her arm or put an arm round her waist rather more frequently than earlier and at least one of the more confident men had invited her to join him for a swim.

"No thanks, not just now, but you go in if you want to" which he did, after the most rapid elimination of his clothing in the pool house. With a roar he plunged naked into the pool, sending showers of water in all directions, before surfacing with "bloody brilliant, come on you girls, come and show us your breast strokes." The real party had begun. Sarah caught Ray's eye from the pool into the lounge and both grinned. This party was going to be a big success.

Within moments a couple of the women had slipped out of their dresses and jumped into the pool, the one naked and the other wearing the tiniest pants which followed her to the surface of the pool, apparently of their own volition.

As was intended, the initial leap into the pool pierced the cocoon of manners encasing the gathering and very soon couples, who had been eyeing each other up across the room, were moving around at determined pace to take up the unspoken invitation, as their original partners did the same.

One or two women began conversations of clearly a more intimate nature with one another and some began kissing and caressing the arms of their chosen companion. It seemed those ten thousand messages had been zinging round the room to great effect and were now being developed at some pace.

Although a few of the men remained standing hand in pocket, chatting to one another whilst keeping a keen eye on proceedings, none of them displayed same-sex inclinations.

Pamela was not altogether surprised nor displeased at developments. In fact she became quite excited despite having restricted herself to only a second glass of champagne. This was the stuff of books and movies, but here she was witnessing at first hand - pure Hollywood, but in Northamptonshire.

Just then she noticed The Bitch in one corner of the large reception room, her head thrown back on a shirt-sleeved man behind her, her arms clutching the upper arms of the man in front of her. Pamela gasped inwardly, this was too much. She spun round and headed out to the pool.

At first everything seemed calm around the pool. There was nothing seemingly unusual about the naked shoulders of various couples dotted about the fringes of the pool. But on closer review it was clear to Pamela that they, too, had entered upon more than social intercourse. One lone man was coursing about the pool rather akin to a young male animal seeking to join in the activity of his pride or school and constantly being rebuffed - at least in a light-hearted manner and without requiring to prove his superior masculinity as in the animal kingdom.

Other couples were sitting close in the pool house and around the pool itself enjoying the action in the pool or their own individual moments of arousal. One couple stood up and, arms entwined, strolled back into the house and headed for the stairs.

Such social niceties as had been apparent in the early stages of the Barnes' soiree had all but disappeared by now. The priorities had become finding one or more partners, a drink, a comfortable spot - private to a greater or lesser degree, it didn't really matter - and the chance to sensually explore another human being, or two.

A few diehards were clustered around the gaming tables, but even there the female hands seemed to be massaging more than male egos.

Pamela was experiencing something close to a slow-motion intake of breath as she looked first one way and then another, from the pool to the lounge and back to the pool house. The place was transforming into an intense interplay in sporadic groupings, under water, on chairs, sofas, tables and the thickly-carpeted floor itself.

This was partying at a level and an intensity that was way beyond her previous experience in the woods and little houses of Cranby.

She did not notice The Prince step up just behind her. He too had been watching events around the pool but he had also begun to focus on this mesmerising young woman who had an attractive naivete in her body language. He moved in.

"This is your first time, isn't it, my dear ?" he murmured in Pamela's ear. Simultaneously his arm slid around her slim waist and took her comfortingly into his side. Without waiting for her inevitable answer, he continued: "It all looks a bit frantic, doesn't it. But it's just friends having fun.

"Surely you are not a virgin?" he asked, more as a statement than a question. Pamela turned into his arms. She felt good and her anxiety was evaporating rapidly. He smelt as attractive as he looked and she lifted her eyes to meet his. Close up, they were startlingly blue and the laughter lines were clear in his assured smile.

"I think yes and no are the answers to your questions," she said steadily. " This is my first party at Ray and Sarah's and it certainly has become a lot of fun." Unconsciously and unselfconsciously she had pressed all the right buttons for the Prince. He could barely conceal his excitement at having hit on quite the most exciting woman at the party - young, very attractive, an ingenue with poise, a cool challenge for a worldly man on the verge of sexual boredom. Here, indeed, was almost the perfect conquest. Not a virgin, in truth, but a potentially brilliant pupil.

"Let's find somewhere a little quieter," he continued sotto voce, as he steered Pamela through the various couplings in the lounge. They found a small sofa in the entrance hall. He was in no hurry. This was a moment to savour - the beginning of the chase, the anticipation of the 'kill'.

Pamela was anxious about her role as hostess but his soothing voice pressed on steadily. At one point she caught the passing eye of Sarah, who smiled approvingly as she glided up the stairs with a couple, he greying but still vigorous and she tiny, waif-like, almost a child at first glance, but in reality an exquisitely-formed woman of considerable style.

The Prince, Alexander Palmer-Keening, fixed his blue eyes on Pamela from a matter of inches away on the small hall sofa where they had achieved a measure of privacy as the party music and activity grew in decibels and fell in fabric coverage of the assembled bodies.

"Shall we talk a little more in a quieter place, upstairs perhaps ?" He spoke softly but firmly. Pamela was almost mesmerised by the strength of his presence, his look, his feel, his masculinity. But she remembered that she was Pamela, performing a function at this party and playing a part among the revellers.

She re-called Sarah's words that strongly implied the girls could enter into the spirit of the event once it was under way and she also took note of her new friend Giselle's remark that the tips could be extraordinary if a girl looked after the guests - so to speak.

But she was in turmoil. This man, 30 years or more older than her, was so attractive, so refined and elegant, there was an inevitability about the situation that thrilled her. She took Alexander's hand as they stood up together and headed across to the stairs. After all, as he had said, it would be 'just a little fun.'

And 'just a little fun' was exactly what the Prince offered - a few affectionate kisses and his assurances to Pamela that he would love to 'take her under his wing' and introduce her to more of the significant guests in due course.

After no more than a pleasant, private conversation, he finally murmured: "Are you alright, my dear ?" Without waiting for a reply and taking her satisfied smile as agreement, he continued: "Let's check out the rest of the party. My guess is that it's winding down, so maybe I could drive you home, if Sarah permits ?"

It hardly took a moment for both to resume their posture and they left the room just as two ladies, arms entwined, stepped into the doorway.

"Excuse me, ladies" purred the Prince as he led Pamela gently but firmly across the landing towards the stairs.

Pamela broke off and smiled at the Prince. "Excuse me, while I pop in here as it is free," she said, slipping into the bathroom to make necessary adjustments to her look and touch up the make-up.

Her smile remained as she peered into the mirror and saw the beginnings of a transformation from eager girl to young woman. She had passed some sort of threshold back there in the room with the Prince, and she had enjoyed every moment of it – the intensity of her feelings and the elation of being free to be an adult. He was a nice man.

She stepped resolutely down the stairs to resume hostess duties for a few moments while the Prince went to find Sarah and bid his farewells. As she moved around the ground floor of the house she found guests gathered in groups as before but this time rather more casually dressed and sharing conversation like the lovers many of them had become during the course of the evening. There was much laughter, touching, kissing and making of certain arrangements going on.

Others were wandering smilingly under the influence of the evening and the champagne, scarcely dressed, in search of both clothes and partners. Pamela was amazed at the scene, although her incredulity had a degree of coolness and detachment after her own indulgence upstairs. No longer was she the ingenue waitress, yet nor was she the sophisticate that she aspired to be……………………

The Prince returned, smiling in turn, and said: "I'll take you home, if you would like to get your things. " As he spoke he pressed a thick pad of notes into her hand unseen by anyone near them.

"There's £100 from Sarah and a little extra from our friends – and me. You've been the perfect hostess this evening, my dear. Well done."

Later, at home, Pamela counted out £160 in bank-notes. She stared in mild disbelief at this outrageous fortune before packing the money into her building society book. Crikey, if it was going to be that much fun to earn that money she was heading for some good times. She was still smiling when she fell asleep.

Chapter ten

Despite their strikingly different looks and personalities the brothers Leake were firm and close friends as their respective careers began to unfold. Michael proved a resolute if unspectacular journalist who quickly established a reputation for delivering the goods - on time and very much in the fashion demanded by his superiors.

He had moved on from local journalism within five years and joined the diary page of a leading national newspaper. Again his quiet determination and ability to mingle with a variety of social cliques brought a steady stream of good contacts and amusing anecdotes ideally suited to his outlet.

It was certainly no handicap having a brother zooming around the underbelly of the popular music industry, fixing this, promoting that and getting involved with a great deal of the other. Jeremy was able, very discreetly, to point his brother towards some useful leads.

Michael had entered journalism on a set of negatives rather than as a pre-determined and well-argued ambition. The law, his father's profession, held little appeal. Mingling with creative people at or near the top of their chosen career in the arts of one sort or another had some superficial attraction, but those that he had met during his childhood at his father's occasional dinner parties were, almost to a man, devoid of much charm and driven by a tankful of narcissism, which he found, even in his tender years, distinctly disagreeable.

He had an outside chance of getting a university place at one of the more acceptable provincial universities, to study English. His 'A' level grades were rather borderline but had he pushed hard enough, doubtless his parents would have found a way to press some buttons or pull some levers.

But Michael had a strong urge from his inner 'voice' to go forth and find work to earn his keep. He felt that, even though he had won a scholarship to his minor public school and thus had saved his parents many thousands of pounds in fees, he should start to make his own way.

The mere fact of attending such a school required considerable support with uniforms and equipment and Michael was not one to take anything on offer without feeling some small obligation to re-pay - a somewhat working-class ethic, given his assuredly middle-class upbringing.

His father kept regular hours in general, despite the glamorous and sometimes unpredictable nature of his business, and Michael resisted the notion of being required to be present at a certain time on a certain day simply to please others or to meet some absurd tradition. The very thought of working in a place like a bank or a building society was complete anathema to him - 'thou shalt enter the premises no later than 8.45 a.m. in order that doors may be opened for business on the stroke of nine o'clock' - Dickensian to say the least.

The feeling that financial institutions were peopled by robots, some only marginally more pleasant than others, was to stay with him throughout his life.

No, he wanted to do something that promised a different day every day, where time was relevant but where the individual made a difference. That, and a natural ease with the written word, led him to the offices of the Portsmouth Evening News, where he stood before the rotund, bewhiskered and very bald E.A.Parkinson Esquire, the very model of a Dickensian editor in his leather-trimmed round, swivelling seat, desk awash with galley proofs, and a lugubriously studious gaze.

Clearly his responses to the editor's artfully-crafted questions sufficed and within a matter of days he was delighted to receive a letter on the newspaper's black, heavily-embossed headed notepaper, from the aforementioned E.A.Parkinson Esquire (he never did discover what the initials represented) offering him indentures as a trainee journalist for £100 per week.

Michael was ecstatic and quickly settled into the newsroom with a number of other young starters. They all attended college one day a week to learn the academic background of newspaper practice, law in journalism and Pitman's shorthand writing - a topic, rather like Latin at school, that Michael felt he would never fathom but in which he would eventually excel and use, to one degree or another, in the most unusual situations. Michael would find it remarkable the number of occasions on which he was able to take a note of proceedings, which no-one else could read.

Michael's first two or three years of journalism were to teach him values and give him experience which helped to form his character more than he may have realised at the time.

Sitting in the press box at the local magistrates' court was a profound shock. The wearisome way in which much of the business was transacted - shifting all the 'drunk and disorderlies' out of the way before the meatier cases came up - somewhat shook his idealistic notions about fair trials and everyone being equal before the law.

Very quickly he realised that rogues were rogues, everyone knew it and even the rogues themselves expected to be treated like one by the magistrates who doled out small fines, an occasional day or two in the cells and a firm admonition to behave.

But there had been a murder in town and Michael was in the press box when the accused man was brought before the magistrates for a preliminary hearing prior to the case being transferred to the Assize court in Winchester.

He was profoundly struck by the rather naive impression that the defendant, the accused man whose allegedly appalling deeds were to be outlined by the prosecuting lawyer, looked so absolutely normal. He could have walked down any street unnoticed.

Michael had yet to come to terms with man's inhumanity to man. He had little time to consider such a philosophy as he had 500 words to phone across to the news desk for the first edition of that evening's paper.

Later he was to see, with some pleasure, the billboards around the city 'Hayling Murder: Man in Court' and know that he was the reporter of that story. It was a pleasure, a small satisfaction that was never to leave him in the way of reporting or interpreting the news for a newspaper audience.

Although he was confronted on a daily basis with the mundane, the procedures and protocols of life in a provincial city, he enjoyed the status of a journalist, a newsman, the man at the scene - even if it was only a meeting of the county council planning committee.

That status had its advantages too, for a young man about town. There was a steady stream of invitations into the newspaper for most of the social events, and the older married guys were rarely inclined, or required, to take up some of the less than stellar opportunities which did not involve the local great and good.

Especially welcome to a young chap out to break his sexual duck, however, was the invitation to the local nurses' home for a party. "Even you can't fail to score there, Michael," was the cry from several quarters of the male-dominated newsroom.

There is a mythology that convent-educated girls and nurses are inordinately interested in the baser aspects of human relationships. Michael mused that perhaps the strictures of religious propriety and separation from the male species did it for the convent girls, and maybe the need to shed modesty in the face of dealing with the human body did away with nurses' reluctance to hide their more obvious feminine features.

The joke among the boys from the newspaper as they headed for the nurses' home was what excitement they might generate with a convent-educated nurse !

Michael's evening ended in the back seat of his friend's Morris Minor in a desperately cramped fumble with a nurse, avidly watched by his colleague whose fanatical adherence to the Highway Code's demands on looking in the rear-view mirror were above and beyond necessity.

His relating of the episode to Jeremy later brought snorts of derision from his elder sibling who casually noted that on the same evening he had been approached by an attractive brunette in a London night club who took his arm and said: "OK, I suppose it's your turn tonight."

Michael was aware of a measure of frustration, almost literally, that Jeremy was pursuing a path of pure hedonism in his chosen career while he, Michael, seemed to be stuck in some sort of teenage time-warp.

Jeremy's progress seemed effortless. He charmed everyone who met him and he was adroit at handling stars and management alike, which persuaded his record company bosses to settle his vast expenses promptly and to turn a blind eye to his persistent arrival at work just before lunch after many a night that concluded beyond three a.m.

But Michael stuck to his task doggedly and enjoyed his steady and unspectacular progress. Journalists as a breed tended to be interesting if sometimes bombastic people - but they always had plenty to say about the immediate. He liked being swept along in this tide of certainty.

Michael's awareness of the differences in personalities, looks and attitudes with his brother was slowly growing.

Chapter eleven

Jeremy sat back from the table in the Brown Derby restaurant, eyeing Jennifer insouciantly, the one ankle resting on the other knee, leaning back, his sports jacket fallen open to reveal a fine blue silk tie and a decently flat stomach.

She decided that proactivity was the order of this particular meeting - anything to cover up the disquiet she had been experiencing since Jeremy's strong hint at a relationship with her late husband, of which she had been completely unaware.

"So, Jeremy, you said you had been to one of our parties in Chiswick. That must have been at least ten years ago."

"I guess it was. My life has been a bit of a mad social whirl - you know the rock'n'roll business - no rules, no boundaries and time really does fly when you're having fun in different time zones. Sometimes I think it's on different planets.

"But I've made a habit of keeping a diary of sorts, mostly places, people and dates - more of an aide-memoire than a written conscience. Time passes so quickly yet I remember people very well. It's my job, to run as wide a network as possible. You never know who is going to prove useful - a politician here, a hooker there, and occasionally even a television producer."

Jeremy looked Jenny steadily in the eye as he spoke the last few words. He felt that he had scored a telling blow in the Polo Lounge and he guessed that she was not aware of her husband playing away for that particular team. But Jenny was in full control of herself. The early innuendo had shocked her and she felt she had only partially succeeded in concealing her momentary discomfort at their earlier meeting.

"I got to know Martin from that party of yours. We had lunches and dinners over a period of time - hardly a relationship, not even a friendship as such, more a mutually satisfying coming together" said Jeremy, relishing his provocative choice of words.

"We were useful to one another, as is so often the way in the media world. Strangely I don't think I ever met you again after the first party but Martin did tell me quite a lot about you, including the fact that Jennifer is not your real name - at least not the name you grew up with.

"You seem to have been quite a girl before you married Martin. From what he told me you didn't slow down too much during the marriage, either. Not that he was a paragon of virtue, was he !

"So, are you still a party girl ? Do you still like to go out to play ?"

"I'm not sure, Jeremy," replied Jennifer cautiously, "that a brief, er, friendship with my late husband entitles you to ask such personal questions of a lady. I enjoy being with my friends and seeing off a bottle or two of wine over dinner, but then who doesn't ?"

"What's your definition of friendship, then?" persisted Jeremy. "How quickly does a meeting become a liaison, a liaison a dalliance, a dalliance an affair? All on the same day ? All with the same man ?"

There was a real menace about Jeremy as he pressed these questions. This is getting out of control, thought Jennifer as she fully realised the implications of what he was saying.

"You have a curious way of seducing women - if that is indeed what you are trying to do" she said coolly. She was falling apart inside. This young man was dangerous but he was also attractive and the danger made him exciting. She was pleased at her manoeuvring of the conversation.

"Why don't we order some food and get to know each other a little better," she added, almost back in control. The initial thrusts and parries of the dinner had been more forceful than Jenny would have liked. She now understood that this young man was more significant than many she had met, and yet her style was to linger a little on the chase............

Jeremy accepted the opportunity to relax his own style. The stewardesses may have been fun but this was a woman of substance - a sophisticated and experienced personality who was beginning to fascinate him. If half the things he had discovered about her were true then he could be in for the adventure of a lifetime.........

Their conversation pitched back and forth across the table, animated as a duel led by epees rather than sabres, a muted enquiry here and a witty repartee there. Both enjoyed the rhythm of their dinner joust, the banter between two attracted people.

Jenny could feel a drawing towards Jeremy. Here was an admittedly young man without perhaps some of the sophistication that she had become accustomed to, but with a flair and a freshness that was often missing in her own generation on the masculine side.

She was more and more putting aside that he was something of a mystery man, who seemed to know more about her than she about him, and therefore was slightly dangerous, and more and more feeling that she should know him better in a physical way first before sorting out the conundrum that he presented.

Jeremy was increasingly exhilarated by this woman who looked fantastic in a designer dress clearly fashioned to showcase her sexuality – scooped neckline revealing much of her tanned breasts, a halter neck and a very low cut back showing smoothly inviting skin curving down to her rounded bottom.

The food came and went almost unnoticed and the wine added its potency to the mix of expectation and uncertainty between them.

It was Jennifer who sealed the bid: "Would you like to come back to my room for a glass of champagne to celebrate a lovely evening? " Jeremy was almost sick with excitement at the thought of having this woman of such cool elegance and experience. So much for the sophisticated young man about town.

Jenny turned in the darkness at the sound and smiled. Next to her, hair more tousled than ever, lay Jeremy snoring very quietly but steadily. Why, she thought as she drew the immaculate Egyptian cotton sheets around her breasts, do men so often fall asleep after making love? Jeremy, still a young man, ranked pretty high on her scale of lovers in the physical prowess category although she mused that he had some way to go in the imagination department. Never mind, there would be time.............

Chapter twelve

It very soon became clear to Sarah and Ray that Pamela was exceptional in the role of hostess/facilitator and her potential as a public relations professional was obvious. They wasted no time in offering her a permanent, if junior, position in their thriving regional communications company.

Pamela in turn was thrilled to be considered as a PR person although she was still some distance from appreciating all that the position required. Still, the shorthand and typing were a very good start.

She had met many of their clients at the first party which she helped to host but that was pretty much a blur of faces in her memory. Now she had to study each one, their business, and their communications strategy. Heady stuff for a young woman in her 20s.

Ray Barnes took Pamela to lunch to acquaint her with some of the diverse clients his agency serviced.

"You need to get up to speed on the client list as quickly as possible. It's essential to understand very clearly what the objectives of the client are; how they are proposing to achieve them and then what strategy to employ to help them get the right kind of public acceptance and reputation.

"Of course, a lot of this will become clearer as you get into the job and gain experience of the process and the triggers that deliver the kind of outcome that both you and the client are seeking."

Pamela began to see Ray in a different light and she warmed to him. He was acting like the consummate professional that he was, and he was treating her with respect which she enjoyed. She felt safe with him and quite inspired to do her best to start contributing to the success of his venture.

Sullivan Interactive Networks was perhaps a rather ambitious name for a regional organisation based in the Midlands, but it showed a determination not to get bogged down in local issues and an outward-facing aspiration.

The company had grown exponentially in the seven years of its existence as Sarah, on the one hand, schmoozed potential clients with promises of the impossible before Ray moved in and managed client expectations rather more realistically.

Their big break-through had come when they landed the account for Leicester City Council as strategic consultants to the small in-house PR team.

Their portfolio grew steadily as word spread of their achievements within their enlarged community in the Midlands. A small group of models, male and female, booked out to exhibitions and sundry events; a lively advertising agency; a stately home and, perhaps the cherry on the cake, an American industrial giant with interests in the locality.

Ray ran through the client list over this friendly and relaxed lunch. "It's a mixed bunch and they've all got their individual pluses and minuses but it makes for a challenging and varied work-load.

"You will need strength in diplomacy in dealing with some of the characters, particularly the wolves and the chancers - and we have a few of them," said Ray. " Watch out for Isaac Kernow at the council. He fancies himself as a ladies man, God knows why because he's no oil painting." Pamela smiled.

"Eden James at the advertising agency is a wild man, but he's full of action and ideas and great fun to work with. He has a place in the south of France so no doubt he will come up with an invite for you pretty quickly. He has an eye for the ladies, so to speak, so be careful.
"Few people have been more aptly named than Sandy Conn who runs the Starburst Agency in Nottingham. He's old-school show-biz of the more unsophisticated variety but he's busy, pays his bills on time and is always looking for fun out of the shadier side of show business.

Our prize client, if you will, is Clancy Turner of the Bechtel Corporation of America. They are a massive industrial company with fingers in many pies around the world and strong inroads into the American political system. It's a real coup for us to get their business here in the Midlands and it's pretty high-level, serious stuff involving large-scale developments with local and central government.

"You'll need to get much more experience before you can be considered for that account, but Clancy is a good guy to deal with. Cool, calm but very decisive so that account hums along quite nicely. I reckon he will go places eventually in America when he inevitably returns to headquarters, so we must really look after him because there could be some big business in it. "

Chapter thirteen

It had been something of a coup for the record company PR to secure a feature in Michael Leake's column for an American pop group, even one as hugely popular as the New Bees. At the same time, and this had been what piqued Michael's interest, it signalled a broadening of his canvas from more serious issues and personalities into the realms of celebrity.

Michael sat at a long dining table in an imposing house in London's Eaton Square surrounded by the members of the group, various members of their entourage with the whole scenario orchestrated and conducted by their bizarre manager, Mister Showbiz in one of his trademark colourful outfits. A late evening meal had been consumed and the assembly was concentrating on a large-screen projector television set up in one corner of the room showing a film of the concert earlier in the evening at the vast Earl's Court arena.

The New Bees, drilled to near-perfection by their relentless producer-manager, were riding the crest of a new wave of teenage boy bands and, after a lengthy apprenticeship of trudging round clubs and bars in the states surrounding their home state for what seemed like eternity, one of their singles 'caught fire' at a minor Florida radio station and gathered momentum across hundreds more stations in the huge market that is the United States.

Pandemonium was not far behind as the group changed overnight from existing on a few dollars a day to flipping round the United States in a private jet to try to satisfy the overwhelming demand for their music.

Four more huge hit singles in the US had followed the first in the first year of recognition plus three albums with combined sales in the multi-millions. Items of merchandise with the New Bees brand quickly generated millions more dollars in income in what seemed a matter of days - or maybe daze - following that break-out in Florida.

But that's the way it works in America and the rest of the world soon caught up with this latest shooting star for the teenage masses.

So finally, after three years of long-distance hysteria, the New Bees were in Europe, closeted in a grand London house as their base for the tour, and ready to deliver for the 'newbies' as their fans had become known.

The New Bees were five young men, now encroaching on their twenties, including two brothers, whilst the lead singer, and focus of the fevered young fans' attention, was still only 19.

They were the stark contrast to the multitude of sharp, r'n'b black groups, which rarely saw the mainstream in the United States charts, although their work inspired or was blatantly copied by the white artists who had access to the major pop radio stations.

Their African American counterparts were restricted to black music stations with but a fraction of the influence on the major best-seller charts.

The acuteness of this was lost in the UK where indiscriminate screaming teenagers adopted whichever was the hottest act of the moment. Conversely many of America's black acts succeeded to a greater extent in the European charts, where the overt racism and division of the American radio stations were not present, than they were able to do in their homeland.

These were the aspects of the New Bees that interested Michael and formed the basis of his interview - rather more serious than the group members might have been used to. Nevertheless Mister Showbiz barked his orders to the young superstars, instructing them to gather round Michael and answer his questions carefully.

Beneath his shudderingly unnerving appearance Mister Showbiz was more than aware of the value of this exposure in a major European newspaper of considerable reputation.

All the stops had been pulled out by the UK record company for the visit of these American mega-stars with special promotional telephone lines giving out every detail of the band's movements from the arrival at Heathrow, greeted by thousands of hysterical fans screaming at any glimpse of their idols, to the manner of their departure from that evening's concert.

This had been achieved by the group running directly from the stage to a limousine parked with engine running in the wings. As the stars bundled into the car, Michael had been hustled to a second limousine just behind to interview the group at their London base in Eaton Square, complete with indoor swimming pool.

But in the seconds that it took the cars to slip under the rising warehouse-style doors at the rear exit to Earl's Court a bolt of determined fans had rushed, crushed and stripped the cars of any extraneous parts like wing mirrors and radio aerials in their efforts to get at the singers.

Michael, who had only rarely brushed with show-business, was aghast at the ferocity of this adulation which had trashed two expensive cars in a matter of seconds. His interview had been set up by brother Jeremy who had been seeking to translate the New Bees phenomenon to the more mature and established readership that Michael's national newspaper column commanded. He just grinned from his seat in the front of the second car.

The screening of that evening's concert was an opportunity for a merciless critique of the performance by Mister Showbiz. His words were grudgingly accepted by the performing singers, whose ingrained quest for the perfection demanded by their manager was tempered by the familiarity of his tirade. Some of them laughed at the antics of the audience and generally took a delight in the outstanding success that the show had generated. So the criticisms were taken in a good and relaxed spirit.

Michael took out his tape-recorder and note-book which was immediately noted by Mister Showbiz who commanded: " Boys - sit down there and talk to Mr Leake. He's a most important British journalist. Tell him what he needs to know."

The implication of this latter remark was missed by the normally-astute Michael in his surprise at the way the young performers, who were across a dozen pages of every British tabloid during each day of their British tour, were ordered into complete submission by their dominant producer-manager.

Like the super-trained superstars that they were, they were well versed in the art of positive speak, flattery of country, fans, competitors and culture of wherever they happened to be.

Michael was determined to find a way past this deeply-ingrained veneer and discover some deeper sociological context for their success.

Later, as he transcribed his notes at home Michael dwelt on the discipline exhibited within the 'pop family' of the New Bees and how it differed from his own upbringing. His father, Sam, was infinitely more benign than 'Mister Showbiz' and yet discipline had never been an intrusive issue in the Leake household. It rather came naturally with the environment that Sam and Lucy created for their boys.

But soon the familiar doubts about how he felt strangely outside the bond between Jeremy and his parents returned. He decided to confront the issue on his next visit home.

Sam was well used to dramas and bombshells in his daily professional life and so remained poker-faced when Michael explored his feelings over a glass of wine. "Sometimes I wonder if I belong in this family. I mean, I'm very happy and very grateful for all you've done for me but I still have this bizarre feeling that I don't quite belong here. I know it's a really strange thing to ask, but am I really your son ?"

Sam caught his wife's glance as he looked steadily at the young man. " Michael, we've rather been waiting for this moment. Your mother and I made a decision many years ago that we would always tell you the truth and I hope that you feel that has been the case throughout your childhood.

"But equally we are of one mind that if ever a question or a doubt arose about your background - either with you, or through some circumstance - we would remain faithful to that intention and we would not shirk from telling you the truth.

" We adopted you as a baby. Lucy had had a difficult birth with Jeremy and was subsequently unable to have more children. We had been eager to have a large family so in the circumstances we at least hoped for a companion to Jeremy. Some friends put us in touch with a really approachable adoption agency who linked us with the young lady who had given birth to you and was unable to provide for you at the time. She was desperate to give you a good chance in life and we, as I say, were keen to have more children in our family - despite Lucy's problem.

"The needs of the two parties coincided and an arrangement was made for you to join our family. We have grown to love you every bit as much as Jeremy and I tell you that with the utmost truth and honesty. To all intents and purposes you are our son."

"But what about my real parents ?" asked Michael, in a state of some shock despite his lengthy suspicion of the truth that had finally been revealed. He felt no animosity towards these people who were still, after all, his parents-in-fact. But inevitably his mind began to whirl around the identity of his true parents.

"Well," said his father slowly. " That presents us with a certain difficulty. We never met your mother and I have only the sketchiest details about her. There are ways in which you can trace your birth parents, but I believe that she insisted to the agency that her identity was never to be revealed to you. She was young at the time of your birth and I understand that she had not really set out on a career or even a settled way of earning a living.

"So it was formally agreed that you were to be given into our care as your parents unless circumstances similar to today's arose. In this case your mother and I were resolved to tell you the truth and to not stand in your way if you wanted to try and find your birth mother and/or father. We have no details at all about your father and that may of course have been part of the problem.

"And your mother's name may have changed in the meantime. But we will help all we can to find her, if that is your wish."
 Michael struggled to take in so much deeply personal detail and just smiled gently with a rather lame " I don't know."

Chapter fourteen

Pamela put all her energy into 'learning her trade' in public relations, both the social and professional sides. She eased comfortably into the subtle world of influence and calculated strategies carried out with the maximum of pleasure for all parties yet the ruthlessness of a big cat eyeing a herd of wildebeest.

Her progress at Sullivan's Interactive Networks was rapid. As her knowledge and confidence grew so did her reputation as a cool operator and her power within the still-small organisation. And she was not above taking pleasant diversions when on offer.

Wembley arena filled with thousands of screaming teenagers was one of the last places that her client Eden James ranked as a place to be seen but he had overlooked the fact that Pamela was not that long out of her teens. A ticket to see the Hortons in London was sufficient to draw the intriguing young PR woman into a trip to London where he kept a little Notting Hill pied a terre.

The Hortons were just beginning their international career from a string of U.S. hits and appearances on the 'Perry Como" TV show and they were already hot in England. Whether they would become monsters of pop remained to be seen but Eden prided himself on knowing the latest 'in' people and when he wanted to start a new liaison it had to be perfect.

Eden had a very successful Midlands ad agency and was involved with almost all the big businesses in that region. He was good at presentation, never short of a quick argument for his cause, great at thinking on his feet, a tap-dancer in the Sammy Davis junior league.

He was also a notorious socialiser and networker and had quickly marked Pamela's card at Sarah Barnes' parties in Belsingham.

He, like so many before him, was entranced by this self-assured and beautiful girl who knew just how far to tease him while circulating at the party. Eden had inevitably tried countless times to seduce her at the parties, despite the close attention of his waspish wife, so a trip to London was to be his 'coup de grace.'

But Pamela was elusive and proved to be an irresistible tease for Eden who boasted that no woman was safe when he turned on the charm. Eventually he had spotted the Hortons concert on in London where he had just recently taken a shareholding in a larger agency.

The Notting Hill garden flat was intended just as a stop-over for his increasingly frequent visits to the capital, but Eden was not one to pass up an opportunity.

He was already into his first collectible Ferrari, although he drove a top-of-the-range Porsche cabriolet. He was still a well-defined rich, fast and very, very loose man, even though his looks were beginning to show signs of good living with a little extra fold of liverish flesh about his neck,

That he had a fine manor house home beautifully created and maintained by his sharp and aspirational wife Sonia, was of little consequence to the rapacious 'swordsman' James, whose sole purpose in life appeared to be battering his marriage vows into total submission.

Having survived the Horton's 'screamathon', Eden retrieved his Porsche from the car-park at the venue, relieved that the wheels were still intact and the roof not slashed to ribbons, courtesy of the 'hood' based in Wembley.

He whisked Pamela to Morton's in Berkeley Square, Mayfair, for drinks and a late supper. It was a chance for him to show her off to his advertising pals although most seemed to have passed the point of no return in terms of alcoholic refreshment.

Pamela was wide-eyed with excitement at these truly metropolitan sophisticates in the late-night bar, although her natural poise remained in place. She liked Eden. He was full of life and a laugh a minute when in the company of his advertising colleagues – quite unlike some of the dull Midlanders she mostly knew.

But if Morton's was exciting it was as if nothing for the still-impressionable young woman when they hopped back into the Porsche, brought to the door when they left, and flew down to Jermyn Street off Piccadilly to enter Tramp shortly before 1a.m.

Pamela almost hugged herself as she realised that this was the real thing, the kind of life she had read about in magazines and seen occasionally in those self-consciously British pop movies.

Everywhere she looked in the warm, dark womb of the Tramp discotheque were stars, of the pop charts or the movies. Eden stopped to chat to one or two friends in the restaurant before grabbing her and launching himself on to the dance floor for the next two hours, virtually non-stop.

It was teenage ecstasy and Pamela barely noticed the time or even the moment as she careered on through the night with Eden.

Somehow he piloted the Porsche back to Notting Hill and they collapsed into bed. Earlier Pamela had tried to imagine how it would be with Eden since he had made his intentions so clear so often at the Barnes' house. By the time they arrived at his little garden flat, very smart, very chic but very small, she was beyond caring. She was happy and glad to be in the company of such a fast and fascinating man.

They curled up together like spoons in the bed..

Chapter fifteen

Jeremy had been discarded quite early after an inconsequential breakfast during which he had experienced the cool, even chilly, attitude of Jennifer. She was busy with a succession of telephone calls, mostly evidently trans-Atlantic in the late afternoon European time, some with friends and others clearly with financial advisers of one sort or another.

She had dealt briskly with the latter and dallied intimately with the former - especially the men for whom she produced an elaborately flirtatious style, promising a lunch here and a dinner there - perhaps a day out at the races, depending on the diary, darling.

But within Jeremy's hearing she kept the girlie chat to a minimum - plenty of 'can't speak now, but you won't believe it when I tell you what's going on out here.' Jeremy affected a detached manner as he scanned the local TV news and sipped an orange juice. But eventually he got the message and made ready to leave.

"Darling, so lovely to see you. Thank you for a super dinner. I've been there before but it's always pretty good, isn't it?" she said brightly and just a little calculatedly. She wanted this man out of the room fast.

He smiled gamely, almost accepting defeat in the game of bluff and double-bluff but still willing to play some sort of hand. " Let's have lunch when the day settles down a bit ?"

"Oh, I don't think so," came the swift and firm reply. " I've got to meet some chums for tennis and a swim over in the valley and It always ends up in a long session of putting the world to rights over a bottle or three with us girls. Give me a ring sometime and we'll see what the diary says. Bye, darling."

Jenny thrilled inside with the absolute domination she had achieved over young Jeremy, dumping him on the canvas with a casual uppercut.

He acknowledged the blow with a nod and made a swift exit through the mahogany-veneer door of her suite.

Back in his own room, Jeremy slumped in the armchair and set about trying to revise his strategy. He was pretty sure he had located his target - Michael's mother. But she was not making life easy nor giving anything away without a fight - a damned interesting fight between the sheets. The sheer power of her demands and the seeming endless manoeuvres had drawn every last sap of lust from his body - and his mind. He recalled that he must have fallen asleep rather quickly after the love-making and he was disappointed with himself.

That's where he had begun to lose control of the situation. She had not only clearly enjoyed a lively physical encounter with a younger man, but had also neutered his psychological attack over dinner with a full-frontal sexual assault. She had every reason to feel pleased with herself, he mused darkly, wondering how he was being lampooned in the return calls to girl-friends even as he sat two floors below.

Nevertheless the job was barely half done. He owed it to Michael to have a full and detailed report back, now that the initiative to discover his birth-parents was fully under way. Michael's had made clear his anxieties and curiosities to Jeremy prior to this trip to the United States.

The haphazard details they had been able to draw from Sam Leake indicated possible origins in the Midlands for Michael's mother but almost certainly under a different name.

Jeremy decided to call Michael and report what progress he could, although even he drew the line at the more intimate elements of his encounter with this woman Jennifer Hawes…………..Was she ? Could she have been ?

Michael was startled at Jeremy's 'success' or relative success. Jeremy had seemed quite confident that he had tracked down Michael's birth mother, and yet he could not offer any definitive proof. Jeremy decided to bank the phone numbers he had received from Jennifer and return to the UK for further investigation.

Chapter sixteen

Where to begin searching the haystack for this particular needle, thought Jeremy. He was exercised by the challenge he had partially set himself with added pressure from Michael and encouragement from his father Sam.

He had little detail on which to base his research beyond approximate dates and the name of the adoption society, which brought with it no guarantee of further information, especially as he was, to all intents and purposes, not a blood relative of any of the cast.

But somewhere along the way he heard about a young PR woman with slight show-business connections in the Midlands who disappeared abruptly at roughly the same time as Michael had been born and had never been heard of again.

His informant was an ex-girlfriend from a disappointing relationship who failed in a creative career and turned to property investment instead. During a brief and rather cold conversation - the liaison had ended badly - she recalled renting part of one of her houses in St Ives in Cornwall to a young woman from the Midlands who seemed to be both distraught and pregnant.

Nevertheless a lead is still a lead and it was by far the best he had managed too uncover in the first weeks of his investigation. So he turned to his contacts book to see where it might lead him.

With only a vague geographical reference to set him off, Jeremy sat in his Chiswick flat dredged up what he knew, or rather who he knew, in the Midlands.

Within moments he was flicking through his well-thumbed phonebook, carefully and uniquely cross-indexed under name, city, business, occupation and usefulness. It was a system with which only he was familiar, but it gave him access to the ever-expanding database of his contact book within seconds of an idea coming to him.

And so, in this situation, he was looking at 'L' for Leicester, which led him straight to the name of Sandy Conn, the one-time premier agent in the greater Nottingham area who had tried - and almost succeeded - in foisting a New Seekers-style boy-girl band on him.

Sandy's fifteen minutes of fame and power derived from the latin-look lothario he had discovered singing in a small club in Kettering and from whom he had made a more than modest living around the working men's clubs of the Midlands and North of England.

But Sandy's style lived up to his name and he was never the smartest egg-cup on the table. So busy was he collecting the 40% or so of the booking fees of the talented balladeer that he neglected to tie the boy down to more than a flimsy management contract, and never gave a thought to a bigger stage for him to perform on.

Enter top London manager who snapped up the young man, changed his name, groomed him and put him into a recording studio with a gilded producer and a song for the charts. Result ? A number one hit in England and America and a career for life. Sandy was happy, though, with his 2% royalty for the first album.

Jeremy felt amused as he recalled Sandy's social style - surely a contradiction in terms. Sandy used his local infamy to keep at least one mistress and a fair string of other young women anxious to meet something famous. Or perhaps that should be a string of fair other young women, considering they tended to be blonde and, regrettably, lacking in personality.

His mistress Jackie, however, was no shrinking violet. Her party trick, which she trotted out with monotonous regularity, was to flash her not inconsiderable breasts over lunch in some of the smarter restaurants in London when her Sandy took her - just the once.

"Jeremy, lad. What can I do for you or how can I do you ?" cackled Sandy on the phone in his inimitable and forgettable way.

Jeremy was interested in party life in the Midlands and recalled to Sandy how he had once taken him to an interesting stag night with, was it the Northamptonshire Knights or something ?

"That's right, my boy, and I introduced you to Ray Barnes. Do you remember? Didn't you go on to one of his parties the following week ? You must remember his missus - Sarah. Blonde, right up front - in fact all up front." He sniggered and slobbered down the phone. Jeremy could picture the older but no wiser agent as he spoke.

Jeremy had, indeed, gone to one of those parties and his mind began to piece together the scene................

He found Ray Barnes in his book under 'R' as well as 'B,' with Sullivan Interactive Networks noted alongside (also filed under SIN) and under 'P' for parties.

He looked up from the book into the middle distance and recalled his last visit, probably five years earlier.

Ray and Sarah Barnes had greeted him warmly at the door of their spacious but irrepressibly provincial home as he stepped from his BMW.

Once inside he swept the scene with a practised eye and acknowledged one or two enquiring glances from men and women. He decided to give this bash a couple of glasses of champagne to see what developed. But then his eye rested on a tall, distinguished looking man, stooping slightly with age but still with a sophistication beyond present company. He had the air of royalty, thought Jeremy.

His eye was met by this ageing but still impressive man who quietly excused himself from the small group to whom he had been talking and made his way towards Jeremy.

"Hello there, Alexander Palmer-Keening. This your first time at Sarah's ?" Without waiting for a reply he took Jeremy's elbow and began to steer him through the crowd. "Let me show you round a bit. There's usually some, er, interesting people here and there's always plenty of lovely girls to keep you fizzing.

"Unfortunately things are not quite what they used to be, so many of the leading lights of these occasions have moved on to brighter and more lucrative lives. But we do what we can to have a good time, especially when there are attractive young men like you around.

" What's your fancy ?"

"Well, I've just walked through the door and I'm taking in the sights at the moment. Presumably you are an old hand at these parties ?"

"I've been coming to these do's for, I suppose, more than twenty years come to think of it. I think my time with the ladies is probably past by now, but I still have an eye for a fine young man. No sense in wandering around the point. That's the reason for Ray and Sarah's gatherings – attractive and influential people meet similar. Here, let me get you another drink. You simply must see the gardens here."

With that the Prince led Jeremy firmly from a tray of drinks held by a beautiful brunette with a velvet gown slashed to leave little to the imagination. Jeremy paused momentarily, but he understood Alexander's intentions and let himself be moved on by this gentle and still attractive man to the darker corners of the garden beyond the floodlit pool.............

This rather overt yet refined introduction to the Northamptonshire social scene was quickly over and Jeremy's thoughts turned back indoors. He politely extracted himself from the Prince's failing grasp, straightened out his silk evening dress suit and headed purposefully back to the drinks dolly.

As he entered the house he was confronted by two well-presented women, certainly beyond the first flush of youth, but definitely not beyond the pale of possibility. Both wore expensive dresses designed to show their remaining attributes to best effect.

The one with jet black hair spoke: " Hello ? I'm Tessa and this," gesturing to a platinum blonde struggling to stay within a plunging neckline, "is Diane. We saw that old rou Alexander trying to capture you and we thought we should rescue you, because we would like to get to know you much better."

With that the two women linked arms with Jeremy and moved him just as firmly through the throng to the stairs and quickly into an unoccupied bedroom. Jeremy amused himself in a flash with the question 'is this rape?' as Tessa took charge of unbuttoning his shirt and unzipping his pants. Diane, meanwhile had stepped out of the remains of her dress to reveal a thriving figure and a tiny pair of pink gingham panties trimmed with lace.

She spoke for the first time: "I don't think I'm going to be needing these, am I……………?"

Chapter seventeen

Eden James became an intermittent lover for Pamela. She saw through his garrulousness and some of the more embarrassing moments of this self-taught 'Eastender' from the Midlands. And yet his chameleon qualities when in shifting company of varying degrees of business importance, made her smile.

But above all his irrepressible enthusiasm and energy, which were keys to his business success were also the keys that kept her in thrall. Nevertheless her discretion still ruled the day and, although their mutual association brought her plenty of good times, few people were aware of the extent of her relationship with Eden.

Pamela developed her contacts carefully from among the partygoers and clients, calculating the precise extent to which they might become friends more than professional acquaintances - or lovers on even rarer occasions.

Despite his unpromising appearance, there was an aura of power about Isaac Kernow which was mildly attractive. Sitting opposite him in one of Leicester's smartest restaurants, Pamela studied the man across the table, the chief executive of Leicester City Council.

A slim, small figure, Isaac compensated for his Fagin-like look, slightly hunched shoulders, a permanent leering smile showing his irregular teeth but lighting up his otherwise ugly little face, and wandering hands, with a well-practised charm – for women.

His MO was the quiet lunch and perhaps an afternoon 'meeting' which, his diary secretary would be aware, was open-ended.

His manner, designed to deflect attention from his looks and the desperate comb-over across his balding pate, was to touch the arm or hand and project his version of social courtliness to impress. As a high-earner he exhibited a certain style in his dress – good shirts, silk ties and expensive shoes to complement the well-tailored suits.

That he succeeded to a large extent was evidenced by his office at the council chambers being mostly staffed by attractive women of various generations.

"Well, welcome Pamela to the team. I'm sure we will have a successful relationship to our mutual benefit" beamed Isaac, "my staff will be relying on you for sound advice and leadership."

Pamela had worn a close-fitting satin dress with a scooped cleavage likely to arouse Isaac's baser interests and she casually leant forward every so often as if to catch his every pearl of wisdom.

"Will we have any problem with the full council when we present our strategy ?" she asked with the confidence of one in reasonable control of the situation.

"Don't worry yourself about the Council, that's what I'm chief executive for – to lead them, by the nose if necessary, to good and useful works like getting the best advice to handle their official policies." Isaac leered his boast at Pamela.

"That's very kind of you to say, Isaac, and I'm grateful," said Pamela in full business pose.

Isaac brightened at the prospect of maybe clinching a little extra-curricular activity with this attractive young brunette, balanced and determined in her pursuit of business.

He had noticed her out at a couple of the the Barnes' parties and, once he had managed to give his partner the slip for a few moments, he had moved in like a bee seeking pollen, quickly getting in a lunch invite before anyone realised he was actually talking to the party's most attractive hostess and the latest recruit to the Barnes' agency.

Isaac couldn't resist making his attempt at a coup. "Why don't we retire to a quieter place I know round the corner – the Hotel Belmont. I have an apartment there for more private meetings." His lips smiled lasciviously but his eyes implored Pamela for a favourable answer.

"Oh, Isaac, come come. This is Leicester, not Hollywood, and I'm certainly not climbing on a casting couch with you " said Pamela, not unkindly and with a boisterous laugh, which effectively dismissed Isaac's clumsy pass.

But for Isaac it was actually sufficient that people at least had the impression of a liaison with Pamela – a circumstance that satisfied his ego yet remained easily denied. The rest was in his head.

Chapter eighteen

The Prince proved an able master for Pamela. Containing his delight at connecting with such a young prize he set about assiduously grooming her for a life of pleasurable success. And she was a more than willing pupil. Theirs was no Master-submissive relationship, Pamela saw to that.

Sarah beamed with satisfaction at the mere mention of her name. Pamela had quickly become a star attraction at the parties and was already making a strong impression with her work at the agency, yet she remained both youthful and extremely discreet. She never drank too much, nor did she disclose in open conversation the pleasure she gained from 'a little fun' with the party guests.

Pamela injected a new pace, a new dimension to the proceedings. She was beautiful, but not so much to irritate the other women, and she was tempting, almost without exception, to their menfolk. Pamela mixed the cocktail according to her particular appetite for the evening.

Pamela remained under the protection of her self-appointed patron, the Prince, as she developed her presence at the parties, initially in the guise of hostess, then a rapidly-aspiring PR person and an ever more sophisticated playmate in her widening circle of acquaintances.

One of her first client contacts was the Duke of Avonborough, or Jamie. A very distant cousin of the Queen, he was the very epitome of the aristocratic set – lots of land, no money, but a lifestyle that flew in the face of reality and included plenty of hunting, shooting and fast cars.

Pamela joined his shooting parties occasionally in company with the Prince and had enjoyed one or two dinner parties at his 'seat' – Winscombe Hall in the East Midlands.

The Duke was a happy, gregarious fellow, at home on the racecourse or in the casino when 'in town.' Pamela liked him immediately. There was nothing much complicated about him, apart perhaps from his wife, the ruthlessly social-climbing Petronella. Rocket science was not even on nodding acquaintance with his intellect.

Jamie was witty and relaxed away from his wife and thus good company for his many male friends and a possible catch for quite a few of the women who invariably were drawn to his charm.

He had become enamoured of Pamela at the Barnes' parties and had cautiously, shyly even, invited her, accompanied by Alexander of course, to his country home. This was life on a scale that Pamela had never imagined having grown up in her little cul-de-sac off the main road through Cranby.

In the vast spaces of Winscombe Hall Jamie was able to legitimately draw Pamela away from the crowd that always inhabited his shooting parties and he set upon a daring plan – to invite her to his private study. Perhaps that might convey the message to her that he was unable to put into words.

Pamela was hugely impressed by the Avonborough study with its double-aspect windows over-looking the beautifully-manicured grounds around the house. But Jamie wanted even more for her to be impressed by his truly private study, which was through a locked door on one side of the room.

He was hoping for the shock effect to melt what he supposed might be Pamela's inhibitions when she discovered the intensely sexual nature of the d cor and contents of this little room with its large television screen and video recorder.

Instead she left him speechless: "Wow, Jamie. What a great room. Is this where you come to masturbate ? Gosh, I've never seen some of these books before. You racy old devil. Did you put this together or was it inherited from a pornographic parent ? " she laughed and pushed away his childish effort to grab her by the hand.

"Come on you big pussycat, let's get back to the shooting party." And thus collapsed the former public schoolboy aristocrat's clumsy effort at seduction

Nevertheless Pamela remained tight in his affection and was frequently consulted on the public relations aspects of keeping Winscombe Hall open to the public. And the Duke was always remarkably prompt with his Coutts cheque to settle her account. But, beyond a little giggly hand-holding, Pamela never came close to indulging the aristocratic aesthete further.

Chapter nineteen

Jeremy decided to give Sarah Barnes a call. Belsingham had a highly-recommended restaurant in the High Street to which he was delighted to invite her to lunch.

He arrived a few minutes early and was immediately directed to 'Ms Barnes's usual table, sir.'

He had absorbed the atmosphere and the menu of this surprisingly classy place when, fashionably ten minutes late, in swept Sarah Barnes, pushing 60, but still packing a heavily made-up punch. She gestured aside the phalanx of waiters and managers that had materialised at the door upon her entrance and smiled broadly at Jeremy.

"Now I recognise you," she lied. "How are you ? What are you up to these days ?" She had adopted the opening gambit of one who is barely interested but slightly intrigued.

She still had a certain allure. She was simply dressed in a straight black skirt and a white shirt with just one too many buttons undone to accommodate her darkly tanned bosom, and a simple gold chain around her untidy neck.

Jeremy quickly re-established his credentials of a man about the music business and not some odious agent provocateur from the News of the Screws, which enabled Sarah, wiser with years, to relax a little.

"A little champagne ?" helped her to ease up even more and comfort herself in the blanket of charm that Jeremy wove around her. It didn't take much more effort on his part to start the ball of reminiscence rolling.

"Oh yes, we've had some wonderful parties. Of course, it's a business for Ray and me, promoting one client or product to another and to the media – sort of networking before the word was invented, really.

"There's very little going on in this county that we don't know about – and a lot more besides ! But that's the point, don't you think ? To get things settled in a private, friendly way. I think anyone who means anything in Northamptonshire has been to one of our little soirees at one time or another."

Jeremy smiled patiently. But what happened to all the people – do they still come or have some moved on ? He indicated that, for once, his interest lay solely in women, especially the singletons and, perhaps, the girls who had acted as hostesses at Sarah and Ray's 'events.'

"Ah well, we've had so many girls come to our parties. Some only last the one but others……well some of them have a great deal of fun. Very discreet you understand because that's what we've always insisted upon. But very few have what you might say 'conquered the scene.' "

"There was one, I recall, who was head and shoulders above the rest. She came to us very young, almost too young, but Ray recommended her and his taste in girls is pretty keen. She was young but she had an air about her, somehow more worldly than her age but na ve and vulnerable at the same time. You could almost call it star quality. She was intriguing."

A "teensy" glass more of champagne was required. It seemed to keep the flow of memory going and Jeremy was happy to oblige. But there was a danger that the flow of champagne might overtake Sarah before she reached what Jeremy might term the climax.

But Sarah had a different sort of climax in mind. She rambled, she smiled, she touched his arm, she drank another 'teensy glass of shampoo' and she took his hand and placed it just above one knee……

" I think I would like an escort home, dear. Ray is away on business for a few days and I might get, you know, lost……." she giggled.

The sex wasn't the worst Jeremy had participated in. Sarah still had a trick or two to teach the young pup and, beyond the wrinkles, her body held an attractive shape. It might have gone on a little longer hadn't Sarah taken the male prerogative and fallen asleep amidst the rumpled sheets and hastily shed clothes.

Jeremy showered and dressed as she slumbered noisily on the bed. He wondered how he might tease a name from the sleeping form when Sarah stirred.

"Hello darling, you still here ?" she said, one eye open and rather dreamily. " Did I finish telling you about Pamela ? Ooops, I've rather let things out the bag there, haven't I? Well, I think she changed it later….."

"Be a good boy and close the door quietly, please."

Chapter twenty

Michael's piece about the New Bees had opened doors for him in two directions. His more serious current affairs readers had found the non-political column a dose of fresh air from the usual establishment suspects, and younger readers, attracted by the subject, had possibly their first taste of decent written English.

Now he found himself seen as a commentator on wider matters than political current affairs. He was encouraged by his editor to add a lighter, more popular – even humorous – tempo to his work and he found that he enjoyed the greater freedom.

He began to look further afield than Westminster for subjects for his big interview pieces and he even, on occasion, allowed himself a little personal exposure in commenting on events that occurred in his own life.

His star as a writer of note was definitely rising. Not perhaps to the heady heights of polemic as practised by Richard Littlejohn or the unfailingly amusing chatter of an Alan Coren . But he was widely read and accepted as an interesting media voice.

For Michael this was something close to heaven. In his rawest days as a trainee journalist he had attended a deeply rural house fire and was so enthralled with an opportunity to drive the company car back to the office to phone over deadline-beating paragraphs, that he was stunned to be told on his return by his mentor "why didn't you use the fucking phone box over there?"

Despite this, Michael had dreamed of a day when he could earn a living writing pretty much from his own inspiration, and be well thought of in his industry.

And here he was, still just in his twenties, a star in the making. He determined to develop his position with more penetrating pieces based on interviews in which he might just bring out a new insight into well-known people or introduce lesser-known mortals to a wider audience.

Chapter twenty-one

The moment Jeremy had left her room, Jenny dialled another transatlantic call – to Northamptonshire. "Sarah darling, it's...er...Pamela. Long time, no speak."

After the briefest of pleasantries Jenny ascertained that a 'darling young man' had recently visited Sarah and asked lots of questions about her parties in the past. It didn't take an algebraic formula to identify said young man 'he looked like a young Kennedy, so charming.'

Of course Sarah had been absolutely discreet, darling. 'Not my style to mention names, of course'

Jenny replaced the receiver, really no further forward with her enquiries into this young man's background. But for the moment she was really rather satisfied with what he had in the foreground. Time to call Melanie.

"Jen, what on earth is going on out there," said Melanie excitedly. "You sounded like a dog with two tails just now on the phone. Was there a man in the room, so you were rather cryptic ? "

"Yes, of course, darling. To be honest I'm not quite sure what is going on – for once. This really attractive young man came up to me at the pool the day before yesterday and called me 'Pamela.' "

"Good heavens," exclaimed Melanie. "No-one has called you that in living memory. Who on earth is he ?"

"Well, that's what I am trying to find out. It's a bit worrying in one sense because he's quite clearly done a lot of research on me – been to Northampton and so on – and yet all I know is his name's Jeremy, he's trying to solve a problem for a friend, quite what the problem is he won't tell me, and he's got the cutest bum. "

"So you sorted out the physical first ? Go on surprise me," laughed Melanie. "What is he like – apart from the cute bum ?"

"He's not that tall, about five-nine I'd say, but he has a mop of blondish hair and a fantastic smile. Looks a bit like John Kennedy when he was younger. He's slim and just cheeky enough. I haven't been so turned on in ages. "

"You'd better be careful, darling, until you know a bit more about what he's after – so to speak. How old is he, anyway." Melanie continued her giggle.

"Well, the fun and games is not the ultimate aim, that much is clear. But I'm going to pursue this one. It's too good to miss."

"Lucky you," chortled Melanie. "Must go, love, there's someone at the door. Bye."

Chapter twenty-two

There were well-meaning people, nice people, aspirational people, attractive people, sexy people and relatively glamorous people at the Barnes' parties.

And then there was Sandy Conn - firmly at the other end of the social scale. Sandy was a born-again accountant who quite firmly believed that his knack for a glib and pointless phrase had turned him into a major-league entrepreneur.

He represented the rotten underbelly of show-business. He even looked seedy with garishly mismatching clothes of indeterminate design and manufacture, plastic National Health framed glasses and yellowing teeth suffering from an onslaught of cheap cigars.

Even his body had gone to seed. But this did not prevent a certain kind of woman attaching herself to him while his wife remained firmly at the small, cheap but detached home in a less desirable part of Northampton.

His mistress Jackie was as loud as him in appearance and manner. Ray and Sarah's parties were her idea of heaven where she could disport her ill-proportioned body to some small effect while her partner dispensed his ceaseless patter to increasingly disinterested listeners.

Nevertheless, Sandy had fingers in many show-business pies, a fact which kept him in circulation, much to most people's discomfort, and which maintained his supply of second and third-rate 'turns' for exploitation around the working men's clubs of the Midlands.

The Midlands were Sandy's 'patch,' which he guarded fiercely in concert with similarly gauche agents and club managers in other areas of the country.

Pamela did her best to avoid his touch at Sarah's parties but allowed a certain degree of conversation and tolerated his smutty banter because Sandy was useful for all sorts of occasions and the supply of tickets for more desirable shows.

Visually Sandy Conn and Isaac Kernow made a good pair, although at opposite ends of the fashion spectrum. Rather urgent hand-holding and somewhat more was the preferred technique of Isaac Kernow, nothing so smutty as a bald, direct statement in which Sandy specialised.

That Isaac attended Ray and Sarah's parties in the company of his wife's best friend was certainly no impediment to his pursuit of any attractive woman – including Pamela. Isaac was nothing if not discreet to a Machiavellian degree, and he would never be caught 'in flagrante' with her, or anyone else for that matter.

Nevertheless he too had not made it past first base with Pamela, who had become adept at playing such lotharios along for what they might be worth – to her. Isaac had met his match with this young woman's negotiating skills, since her particular charms gave her a head start over him anyway.

Isaac was linked to one of Pamela's inner circle, Eden James, through mutual business interests

Eden was head of the biggest advertising agency in the region and clear in his ambition, having just bought a significant share-holding in a major London agency. Where Isaac manipulated behind the scenes to achieve his objectives, Eden strode in full-frontal to present his case.

It was not difficult for Pamela to succumb to his golden glove approach at Ray and Sarah's parties and after the first fumbling weekend in London, she found sex with him to be instructive and exciting – given that his wife was often in the same building. She liked his persistence too. He had an ability to focus, which clearly had aided the swift progress of his business but was also useful in making any woman feel unique.

Eden was a paid-up member of the back-scratching fraternity in more ways than one and he made sure that Pamela's agency gained plenty of work from his clients, just as he, in turn, worked with many local businesses and councils.

But of the various personalities to which she had been drawn over a year or two of socialising and partying, none exceeded the attraction for Pamela of the sublime American, Clancy Turner.

Clancy was a lawyer working for the mighty Bechtel Corporation of the United States on secondment to the steel company in Cranby – a most unlikely combination of smooth, quiet American sophistication and the grimy, visceral bluntness of the largely Scottish Cranby workforce and management.

Clancy pretty much had it all. He classified himself as an African-American although his blood was mixed sufficiently for him to pass unremarked in personal and professional circles. His father was black and his mother Hawaiian and Clancy seemed to have inherited the finest genes from both.

He was American professional football tall with the sleekest physique to go with it. A bright, white smile lit up his maddeningly regular features topped off with cropped dark hair. The man was a God !

Still only 35 he was already a high-flyer, vice-president at Bechtel and a sometime adviser to the US government on international trade. The combination of looks, power and growing wealth made him irresistible not only to his already-sanguine wife but virtually every other woman who crossed his path.

Clancy took it all in good heart. He had sufficient ego to know who he was and where he intended to go, but he kept it well contained beneath a charm and subtle intellect which served him well professionally and personally.

Pamela was hooked from the first moment that she saw him. He maintained a distance at the few R&S parties he attended although not so few that she didn't notice him.

They became lovers soon after Pamela started working on the Bechtel account. Despite her growing experience nothing had prepared Pamela for the first sight of Clancy naked. He really did have it all ! And he lived up to his advance billing extremely well.

Ride a cock horse, indeed, she mused.

Pamela skilfully blended two roles with Clancy. He maintained a house at Oundle, 20 miles from Cranby, for his more sensitive business meetings and the occasional dalliance for him and his most immediate friends.

Pamela came to know the place well as a comfortable and relaxed venue for her assignations with Clancy, but she kept these were quite separate from her professional responsibilities, which impressed Clancy even further.

There were occasions, of a much more formal nature, when Pamela was happy to act as Clancy's partner and hostess for the evening. She even kept a change of clothes at the house and took care of running the place for him.

Isaac Kernow and his mistress had been guests at the house one evening when Clancy shook hands on a massive deal to develop vast tracts of land between Cranby and Leicester on behalf of Bechtel and some partners. Pamela had moved quietly in the background, being the perfect hostess, directing the chef and two waitresses to fuel the proceedings.

When the guests and staff had left, Clancy grabbed Pamela in the highest of spirits and carried her to the bedroom where he had already installed a fresh bottle of champagne in a bucket of ice.

These were the moments she treasured with Clancy. His strength, his smile, his near-perfect body and his spectacular erection were guaranteed to reduce most women to whimpering submission. But Pamela was not only skilled in the hostessing department, she was well able to control these proceedings just as deftly.

Clancy kissed her deeply and stripped her clothing expertly from her body. He deliberately stretched across her head to reach the champagne.

Clancy popped the champagne without a care for the spillage and began to drizzle it across her breasts and down her belly. He then followed the champagne trail with his tongue.

Pamela thrilled to his forceful touch. Still clutching the champagne he was kissing his way over her body. Then he produced a couple of ice cubes and began to gently rub them around the same places.

The sensation of the cold ice on her most intimate spots was a supreme feeling for Pamela and she abandoned herself to whatever Clancy might want to do next.

Pamela awoke in the early hours, turned slowly in the still-damp Egyptian cotton sheets and smiled to herself, momentarily. The smile vanished when she realised that Clancy had, as usual, crept away from the bed to return home after his 'late meeting.'

She rose and wandered sleepily to the shower where the warm jets of water soon invigorated her body and her mind. She recalled the passionate sex, which had devastated the bed, and she bent to massage her knees, which still retained the pressure of the floor – the floor ?

Her hands passed over her soapy body in much the same way as his had hours earlier. She stepped from the shower and wrapped herself in the comforting, fluffy towels, which she had chosen on his store account.

Pamela surveyed the wreckage of the bedroom, took immediate comfort in the fact that the cleaner would soon arrive to restore order, and dressed quickly in the spare set of clothes she kept in the wardrobe.

Her smile returned when she remembered that she needed to select more clothes at home and pack for a weekend in the South of France……..

Chapter twenty-three

"I want to meet her," said Michael firmly. Jeremy had been reporting his trip to Los Angeles to meet Jenny, or Pamela, and his earlier lunch with Sarah, although he conveniently omitted to mention the dessert.

"Could be embarrassing," countered Jeremy. " She seems a very strong possibility to me but we cannot be certain and we have to be certain. I have found nothing so far to suggest that she has ever had children.

" No, I think I have to take this forward a little more and prise some evidence of kids out of her. No disrespect, bro, but we have to be sure."

Michael rather gloomily nodded his agreement.

Chapter twenty-four

Jeremy stood waiting impatiently at Terminal Four at Heathrow in the arrivals hall. He had been surprised to get a calculatedly sweet call from Jenny inviting him, darling, to meet her flight from Los Angeles. She might forgive him for having left without saying goodbye, but perhaps she had been a little, well, hasty with him.

Jeremy was even more surprised that he had so meekly agreed and wondered what was in store. The BMW was parked conveniently close to the terminal building so his training had kicked in for meeting a VIP. Gosh, was she a VIP already?

Jenny swept out of the Customs hall, porter and baggage in tow and pounced on Jeremy. " Darling, it seems absolutely ages since I saw you last. What have you been up to? No, tell me in the car – you have brought a car, I suppose?"

She chattered on endlessly and mindlessly as Jeremy drove smoothly into West London. The words just flashed past his ears without troubling the brain within. That was too busy trying to get a fix on the agenda this intriguing woman was developing.

"Oh left here, dear" she pronounced, and after a few more turns Jeremy drew up outside a discreet house in Bedford Park, Chiswick. Ah, he faintly recalled the party some years earlier. But what now?

Gamely he unloaded her various suitcases into the hall of the house. " Thank you, darling. Now how about a glass of fizz? I think I left some in the chiller."

Tired she may have been from the flight but Jenny was possibly the finest actress Hollywood had never seen, and she settled beside Jeremy on the deeply comfortable sofa………..

" So, darling, I hear you've been to Belsingham to see a friend of mine. You didn't tell me about that in L.A. Come to think about it you didn't tell me much about what you are after, if you'll forgive the expression," cooed Jenny in Jeremy's ear as she expertly allowed her fingers to play across his chest and thighs. The urgency of the enquiry in her mind was just about the only thing keeping her awake after a particularly turbulent trans-Atlantic crossing, but it was enough.

"So what was all that private detective stuff all about, sweetie pie?"

"You intrigue me, " responded Jeremy slowly and carefully. " I told you in LA that I was trying to solve a problem for a friend of mine – and so I am. When I began to make enquiries on this person's behalf you seemed to figure in a number of the stories I was hearing."

"But who is this person you're working for? " persisted Jenny with all the insouciance she could muster. All the while her heart was alternately sinking and thumping.

She was confident that young Jeremy had not discovered her innermost secrets and the source of her own anguish – even the cause of the major change in direction that her life had taken.

But he was certainly an attractive young man. How much to give ? How much to allow him to find ? There were deep, dark secrets and then there were mere escapades or the usual tedious mishaps in business relationships. There could be all manner of people interested in tracking her down.

"I can't tell you that. It's a matter of great confidence and sensitivity. But it seems our paths have inter-twined more than once. Without realising who you were I was a friend of your late husband and it seems that we also have a common acquaintance in Sarah Barnes."

"Ah," said Jenny thoughtfully. " You went to one of her parties ?"

" I did indeed, and I met several more people who seemed to know you well."

"But why are you doing this Dick Dastardly routine on me ? What am I to you – apart from a gloriously attractive woman, of course," she added sweetly. "How did you get invited to a party in Northamptonshire when you are London-based ?"

" Oh, I get around. I told you I know loads of people in the most peculiar places. And there's few less peculiar, or at least less insidious than Sandy Conn." Jenny caught her breath at the mention of the sleazy entrepreneur's name.

Jeremy did not notice the change in Jenny's poise and ploughed on. " I worked with one of his acts for a while but the guy hasn't got a clue about developing talent. " 'Hmmm,' thought Jenny silently.

"He took me along to one when I was in the area and I must say it was a lot of fun. I met Alexander, he's very charming. I'm sure you must have met him – Alexander Palmer-something, known as The Prince, presumably because of his rather aristocratic manner.

Jenny's eyes were locked on Jeremy as yet more details of her early circumstances were relayed to her by this somewhat exotic young man. God, he'd met the Prince ! How much did he meet him, one wonders.

"I also recall a nasty little bit of work called Isaac. Snivelling little Jew who couldn't keep his hands off women – any women. Apparently he dumped his wife for her best friend and now he dumps on her. Didn't take to him at all for all his slimy charm."

Jenny was nearly convulsed as she realised how close he had come to her former circle of influential friends and admirers.

Mustering up all her cool and reserve, she enquired: " Did you ever meet Clancy ?"

"No, can't say I did. What was he like?"

"Oh, American legal type. I believe they call them attorneys over there."

" No, I don't remember him. What was he – tall, short, fat, old ?"

" Oh, just an average kind of guy. Not particularly attractive, quite young but, of course, very married. I just wondered if you heard what happened to him because he only appeared at Sarah's a couple of times. I assume he must have gone back to the States at some point."

" Sounds as though he made a bit of an impression on you."

"No, not at all. I was just trying to recall any other people from those days whom you might have met. So…….where is all this leading my dear, before I collapse from exhaustion."

Before Jeremy had a chance to continue, Jenny wrapped her arms and legs around him on the sofa and fell into a deep sleep.

Chapter twenty-five

Michael met Jeremy in Morton's club and bar in Berkeley Square. Michael was impatient to find out more about this woman whom Jeremy believed to be his natural mother.

"Look, I'm beginning to build a picture of her early life and she seems to have been a bit of a lad. Don't get upset but she was certainly a party girl when she was 20 or more years younger" said Jeremy.

" But there is no hint of her ever having children. I'm sorry to be so sort of blunt about all this but you wanted me to try and find your mother and I would rather tell you the truth as I hear it, than paint a picture I think you might prefer."

"And I <u>want</u> the truth," said Michael firmly, sounding more like Ed Murrow in his best journalistic posture. "You know, I'm terribly grateful to mum and dad for having raised me, and you've been just about the best brother any bloke could have. But I need to know where I come from – who my parents are, what my background really is. It's beginning to bug the life out of me."

"Michael, I'll keep going. I think this Jenny woman has more to tell me, yet. And I think I might just re-visit one of her pals from the past. Leave it with me and I'll keep in touch."

Michael then sped off from the club in a taxi – bound for another major interview for his column, which was becoming a leading outlet in the press.

Chapter twenty-six

Pamela was happy, excited even, as the plane flew down close to the sea off Nice in preparation for landing at the French resort. There were one or two vaguely familiar faces in first-class – probably heading for their tax retreats in Monaco, she mused.

But she was headed for a lovely weekend relaxing with Eden James at his apparently beautiful modern home in the hills near Mougins. She had seen the pictures, now it was time for the reality, and she couldn't wait.

Eden was waiting in the arrivals hall, wide white smile, tanned face and legs bedecked in rather wildly colourful shirt and Bermuda shorts.

"Hello darling," they chorused and he led her outside to............an open-top 2CV.

"Whatever happened to the Porsche, dear ? Or the Ferrari perhaps ?"

"Nah, too ostentatious in these parts. The thieves check you out at the airport and knock you off on the motorway if they clock a motor like that, or a Rolex. Anyway, I told the missus that I was popping out to the tabac for some snout, so I could hardly take the Roller."

"Darling can we cut out the south London wide-boy routine ? What is your wife doing here? Am I heading for some sort of m nage a trois? Have you told her about me?"

"Not exactly and no would be the answers to that. She insisted on coming over at the last moment and turning it into a week of parties for some of our mates, so it's all a bit difficult. We've got a houseful.

"Never mind, I've got this little place in Cannes – useful for the film festival and Midem when me and the boys want to have a bit of fun. You'll be very comfortable there and I'll take care of business. Don't I always?"

Pamela's tetchy grunt was inaudible in the roar of wind as Eden steered the 2CV at rather more than its recommended speed along the autoroute to Cannes. Her delighted anticipation had sunk to a morose contemplation of hours of loneliness interspersed with a little welcome action. Some weekend in prospect !

Eden dropped her at an apartment block just behind La Croisette. He stopped only to carry her bags in, gave her the keys and then made his excuses and left, promising only to ring her later and fix some dinner.

Pamela wandered slowly around the apartment. It was certainly up to the mark for French style and facilities, even if it lacked a view of the sea. Marble floors everywhere lent it a cool elegance rather at odds with the personality of its owner – or tenant. It was furnished in a minimalist cane and cushion style. A few prints adorned the walls and even fewer books and magazines took a little space under the (cane) coffee table.

She was not amused and unpacked in the major of two bedrooms before contemplating her next move.

Chapter twenty-seven

Jeremy cruised up the M1 towards the East Midlands and turned off at junction 15. Some of the twisting road he had recalled from earlier visits was now dual carriageway so he was able to press on towards Alexander Palmer-Greening's modest cottage in a little village a few miles from the A509.

The Prince welcomed him with his usual elegant style, a little tremulous these days, and gestured him into the small house, tidy but as dusty as befits a gentleman, and decked with photographs of friends and family. The house told Jeremy that the glory days were now well behind the slightly stooping figure who brought him tea and some digestive biscuits.

"Well, there's a time in everyone's life......."began the Prince in response to Jeremy's enquiry. But his answer trailed off as he settled into his armchair and clearly began to contemplate some of the adventures of his more active life.

That was just where Jeremy wanted him to be because he realised that this meeting could be crucial to his 'investigation.'

"Y'know, we had a little fun together, didn't we, dear boy ? And that's what life's about, I think. Yes, there's family and bringing up the children, but we all have to sneak in a bit of fun in between times, don't we ?" suggested the old gent.

"Some more than others, it would seem," said Jeremy pointedly. "I've had my share of good times and met lots of fascinating people. But it's all so transitory, isn't it. Sometimes I think it would be nice to be settled in a house somewhere with a family and a few mates down at the pub. Can't remember the last time I went to a local pub !"

"Tell me, this woman Pamela that you mentioned last time we talked. Who else did she sort of hang out with ? I know you were very close to her, but who else was sniffing around ?"

"Well, I would hardly say 'sniffing around.' She was an immensely popular girl and very clever, too. She did the rounds at the parties but she made sure that her business didn't suffer. Quite the reverse. For every little flirtation, if I may put it that way, Pamela made sure there was some business for the PR company.

"Ray Barnes told me that he had found her at a Knights of Northampton event and was struck by her attractiveness. Always had a good eye for the fillies, did Ray.

"Anyway, he introduced her to Sarah and off she went. In no time at all she seemed to have jumped up the ladder at their company and was pulling in good business. Smart girl."

Jeremy let the old boy ramble on for a bit. He wanted him firmly focused on this Pamela and remembering every detail.

Jeremy pressed: "Who were her major contacts, then ?"

"Oh, she knew everybody who was anybody at one time. The council, the parties themselves, advertising agencies – she was a great friend of Eden James, who has moved to London and is very big in the adverts these days. A real rogue, if you ask me, but she stuck with him. Country shoots at the Duke's place – she was a pal of Jamie Avenborough and his wife.

"Networking, you've never seen anything like it, old boy," grinned the Prince.

"Wasn't there an American lawyer at the steelworks who was part of the scene ?" enquired Jeremy.

"Why yes, of course, he was a big figure in her life – in more ways than one I'm led to believe. Clancy Turner, I think he was called. Clancy, huh, a very American name. Came from the South, I believe. Texas, maybe. Quiet, black chap. You know, very light-skinned but definitely a bit of black in there.

"But she didn't seem to do much at the steelworks. She was just a close friend, a very close friend. He kept a house in Oundle, you know, for what he called his 'late meetings.' It was usually his close mates and a night of poker but there were other little gatherings......"

"Was she involved in those 'other little gatherings' ?"

"Not so far as I know. Her part in that place was more a straightforward mistress arrangement. She supervised it for him. But she didn't get involved with the gambling and the rest. He's moved back to the States with his family, of course. Don't know what he's up to now, but he was always a bit of a high-flier, y'know, working with the government there and things.

"Wouldn't be surprised to see him turn up as President one day. He was a pretty serious guy."

"So what happened between them when he went back ? Did she go over and continue to see him, or what ?"

"Oh dear me no. It was all rather curious and I never quite fathomed out what went on, but there was a frightful stink at the time. She disappeared shortly after. Went away, I think for the best part of a year. Never really came back. That was the end of those days, really. Shame. Soon after she had gone, he packed his bags and, whoosh, he was back in America."

"Now, if you don't mind old chap, I must have a little nap. Stick around. Help yourself to the bar or take a stroll round the village. But I need forty winks."

Jeremy contained his frustration . He seemed to be on the edge of a major discovery, which might open up the Pamela/Jenny story, and yet..........

Chapter twenty-eight

Pamela was sitting outside a hotel on La Croisette – the Carlton, naturally – enjoying an aperitif when a waiter strode urgently across with a telephone "Mademoiselle Gerber ? A call for you."

Scarcely had she time to wonder how the boy knew who she was, than Eden was on the line. " I thought I might find you there. Are you having dinner? Put it on my tab. Look, darling, I'm popping out in a minute for a beer with the boys, so to speak, after we've finished dinner here. So I'll see you in about an hour. OK ?"

Pamela supposed so, rather stiffly, and replaced the receiver. She ordered another red wine and a green salad. After 40 minutes or so she strolled back round the corner to the apartment, her froideur subsiding as she anticipated the arrival of her lover.

Nearly two hours later Eden burst through the door of the apartment, leaving the door open behind him, steaming. He had either had many beers with the boys or rather too much wine with his dinner because he was drunk or as near as dammit.

How the hell had he driven down from the hills in that condition thought Pamela. "There's only one place for you, my boy," she said severely," and that's the cold shower. I'm not being mauled about by some drunk."

He needed no second bidding to hop, skip and jump out of his clothes and drag Pamela towards the shower, which was in a sizeable wet room. She managed to divest herself of the few clothes she was wearing, apart from her pants, and followed him into the wet room.

The shower soon calmed him down into a fiery passion under the warm jet of water. Soon they were laughing, tickling and playing 'catch' with the bar of soap as they moved into heavy embraces.

Pamela sighed and slid down his body to her knees. He gasped and leant against the side wall, water still cascading over the pair of them as she added urgency to purpose and drove his – and her own – passion higher and higher.

He pulled her roughly to her feet and turned her away from him as the water continued to splash and spray over their heads and bodies. She gasped in turn as he entered her and began fucking her desperately.

Pamela gradually eased him back to a steady rhythm and felt her own orgasm gathering. Suddenly he moved her out of the wet room towards the lounge, still coupled. Water began to seep across the marble floor but they were beyond caring. Pamela was blind to the moment, this was just too wild, being pulled around, still fucking. She was laughing and sort of protesting without too much force as he steered her towards a chair.

He fell backwards into the chair still holding her, still coupled to her and snorting "Yes, yes, yes."

Pamela opened her eyes and recoiled in horror. There, inches away from her mouth was another cock with an obvious intent. She yelled: "No" and began to pull away from Eden, but his arms around her waist gripped her tight.

Pamela swiftly took in the scene. The closest cock belonged to a leering Isaac Kernow, his trousers about his knees and his Calvin Kleins supporting his weedy balls. "Come on, dear, let's all have a bit of fun," he sneered.

Behind him stood Jamie Avonborough, beaming and appearing for all the world as though he was looking at a picnic hamper of goodies in Fortnums, and Clancy Turner who had a seriously determined look on his face, the like of which Pamela had never seen before, wrapped in a steely smile.

Neither spoke, but even as Eden continued to pump into her body, Pamela sought to gain control of a terrifying situation. She had no time to consider where the others had appeared from although a fleeting thought reminded her that Eden had left the door open when he crashed in.

In a millisecond she summed up the situation. The men had made their excuses at the house-party to go out for a drink. Instead they had mutually decided, or Eden had suggested, to head into Cannes and have some fun – with her !

There was no time to panic and no future in it either. She was no match for four determined men, tanked up, and clearly ready for some action. Besides she hadn't got a thing to wear, she noted wryly.

In the same millisecond Pamela regained some cool and said: "Hang on, boys, I'll get round to each of you in turn, but don't push me, alright ?"

Isaac was having none of this and he tried to force his penis into her mouth. She slapped him away so he led with his forefinger to try and coax her into his intention. As his finger entered her mouth, Pamela bit down – hard !

He yelped like a scolded puppy and lashed out at her, missing her face as she swayed out of the way. In the frenzy Eden's grip slipped and Pamela jumped to her feet and began pummelling Isaac.

"You dirty, filthy bastard," she screamed. "What do you think I am?" She turned to run away. Two pairs of powerful arms grabbed her instantly and flung her on to the large settee. It was then that Pamela realised she was going to be raped.

She screamed, she fought, but the four men overpowered her and subjected her to every conceivable sexual indignity, one after the other, two together and three together, like a pack of wild dogs. No part of her body was spared this savage attack.

She gave up screaming and resisting, it was pointless. She became numb and almost comatose, not knowing who was doing what to her, which hands, feet and sexual organs were intruding upon her person. Something within her told her to remain calm and wait for the end of this torment, which must surely come.

Inevitably as the men climaxed, maybe for the second or third time, their bestiality subsided and they withdrew. Not one spared her a second glance as they grabbed their respective piles of clothing and quickly dressed.

Someone yelled: "Away the lads !" and they exited slamming the door behind them.

Pamela was too exhausted to cry. After what must have been an attack lasting an hour but which seemed like seconds, she was covered in various body fluids from her face to her ankles, completely battered and bewildered as to how this had happened and why. They were supposed to be friends of hers !

Suddenly her body began to react and she stumbled to the bathroom to be violently sick, repeatedly. She turned on the shower, which one of the men had troubled to switch off earlier before the entire apartment flooded, and stood clutching at the wall as the hot water at least washed the filth from the outside of her body.

Then she began to sob. Great wracking sobs seized her whole body, now wrapped in towels, as she collapsed upon the bed. Eventually she fell asleep still twitching as the sobs slowly, very slowly, subsided.

Sun streamed in the window as Pamela's eyes opened. She was still lying across the bed curled up in the foetal position, her knees close to her chest and the towels still clutching at her body.

She hurt everywhere. Her breasts were bitten and sore. Her thighs bruised and aching. Her mouth felt almost as if her jaw were dislocated and was as dry as tundra. She re-visited the scene, surveyed what had been the sofa and which now had one cane arm broken off and resting on the floor. Almost at once tears began to course down and across the cheeks of her face, themselves swollen from the sustained attack she had endured.

The telephone was ringing, but she ignored it. Her mind began to race over what had happened, who had done it, and what she should do now. Should she go to Eden's house and cause a scene ? No, that wouldn't achieve anything and would just make her look like a slut in front of the men's wives.

They would close ranks and accept their husbands' denials. She would be portrayed as some floozy they'd picked up in a bar and left to the mercy of the local lads.

No, she had to get home and consider how to handle this. She needed her friends, desperately, to help her come to terms with this devastating event.

In between the often-repeated incoming calls, she picked up the telephone and called a cab to the airport.

Chapter twenty-nine

Jeremy gallantly settled Jenny on the sofa and found a pillow or two and a duvet with which to keep her cosy. She had finally given in to the exhaustion of the flight back from Los Angeles.

He sat for quite some time in one of the matching armchairs, large, welcoming and all-consuming with its plethora of cushions, and tried to take stock of his position and the progress, or lack of it, in tracking down Michael's birth mother.

He was almost convinced that Jenny was his target and, though his infatuation with her and their assumed closeness had rather clouded the issue, he just needed the smoking gun, the locking piece to this jig-saw he was picking over.

The Prince had virtually led him to the trough, but he was still unable to take a drink.

Jenny had apparently been lured to the South of France on the pretext of a weekend of pleasure with one of her lovers and had then endured some sort of attack at the hands of whom he knew not. Alexander was not about to break confidences of many years and was far too discreet, even in his dotage, to give away potentially damaging information about friends, or at least acquaintances, of his.

This incident had clearly had a major impact on her life. Within weeks she had resigned from her directorship at Sullivan interactive Networks, packed up her house for rental – and disappeared. Then after about a year, as far as the old boy could remember, she had re-appeared briefly in the East Midlands to dispose of her house before moving to London, leaving the life which had come as near as it could to high in the provinces.

The Prince reflected that Ray and Sarah's parties continued for a while after all this had happened to Pamela but, without her, the heart had somehow been torn out of the occasions and the lynch-pin of this micro-society had been pulled.

One by one the movers and shakers of Northamptonshire society dropped out of the network and the whole momentum and purpose of the enterprise began to fail. Isaac Kernow had got himself elected as MP for Leicester, having resigned from the council under some sort of a cloud.

Clancy Turner disappeared back to the States very shortly after Pamela left the area. The Prince wondered for a while if they were together somewhere, but apparently not. Eden James moved to London and became an even bigger noise in the world of advertising.

Only Jamie Avonborough and Sandy Conn remained, the former managing his estate and still featuring at county gatherings, the latter a worm who turned back into his seedy little Nottingham office hole and the twinkling lights of twilight show-business.

The Prince philosophised, as if it were necessary, that every little pool of society had its time and place. A group of friends and acquaintances form an ongoing network of common interest and feel part of a social process that benefits them and contributes to their expectations and enjoyment of life around business and family.

Inevitably other priorities claim members of the alliance and they move on to other aspects of their lives. So it had happened with Ray and Sarah's parties. Their business of PR and promotion continued but the fizz was decidedly gone without Pamela.

Jeremy started, and realised that he, too, had dozed off in Jenny's armchair. It was almost 3a.m. so he had slipped quietly from the house and drove home.

Jenny fumbled for her watch under the duvet. It was 11a.m. She had been asleep on her vast sofa for close on 12 hours. Waking slowly she pieced together the hours before falling asleep.

Jeremy, yes Jeremy, was here. He brought me from the airport after the flight from Los Angeles. Dear boy. He's so much younger but _so_ attractive, she smiled. Wonder if we could make a couple ? Wouldn't do me any harm toting a toy-boy around town. Make the girls jealous tho' Gloria didn't seem to mind ! And I do think he would play the part well.

Perhaps I'm falling in love – again. It's been a few years and there've been a few distractions along the way but it's certainly a long time since I felt this warm and cosy about a man.

Jenny slowly pulled herself into a sitting position, still clutching the duvet. He must have tucked me in when I fell asleep, she thought incoherently. Where is he now ?

"Jeremy !" she called quite loudly, half expecting his cheery face and mop of hair to spring round the door. But there was only silence. Hmmm, best get up and start to move.

Over a strong cup of coffee in the kitchen, Jenny continued to think about her situation and whether to pull this man in close to her. He was quite a character, funny, very sexy and yet still vulnerable enough to be put in his place when necessary.

She recalled the meeting in Los Angeles when she had become irritated with his persistent questioning. She realised that it was only his personal attraction that prevented her from dismissing him as harshly as she had others before him.

They knew so little of each other – at least, she knew relatively little about him, although he seemed to know a great deal about her. And yet he had still to reveal to her precisely what his agenda really was.

Perhaps it was time to bring this little poker game to a finale. One side or the other would have to turn the cards over. Jenny felt her resolve weaken as her desire for Jeremy welled up inside her. She had only once opened up fully about herself to a man before and that was Martin Hawes with whom she had fallen blindly and instantly in love.

Gosh, it was nearly 25 years ago in real time she slowly realised – not long after the birth of her little boy. Where was <u>he</u> now, she wondered ?

Jenny's eyes had lost immediate focus as she meandered around her memories and her coffee subsided from tepid to chilled.

Chapter thirty

Pamela stared at the doctor, her carefully outlined lips wide apart in a look of astonishment. "But……….,"she stuttered in total disarray. "I can't be !"

"I'm afraid there is no doubt, Miss Berger. You are three months pregnant. Is it possible that you forgot to take your pill around that time ?" said the doctor.

"I can't believe it ! It's not possible," protested Pamela. "I always take my pill – I can't afford to be………pregnant." She almost spat out the word.

As the shock waves subsided Pamela realised that she had indeed forgotten to take her pill. That weekend in France, the weekend of the horror, she had left the pills behind in Northampton. It hadn't been too much of a problem since she knew who she would be sleeping with and it was only a couple of days.

But nothing could legislate for the devastating intrusion into her body, her soul, by those four bastards that weekend. And now this. One disaster after another !

The news prompted a frenzy of activity for Pamela. She dismissed almost immediately the notion that she might have an abortion. She could well afford the right diagnosis and a smooth transition in a private clinic but she was instinctively against the idea, no matter what difficulties it might present for her.

She felt chillingly alone. Her parents continued their unexceptional lives in Cranby and she had always kept in touch. But the chasm of sophistication between the world that she inhabited and theirs made each visit increasingly awkward.

She smiled to herself as she considered her mother's reaction to her pregnancy. Her father had warned her more than once that she was 'looking for trouble, mixing with that crowd.' But her mother would have been more pragmatic, would probably have offered to take in the child herself and raise it for Pamela.

It was exactly the kind of project she would relish, giving her an obsession to keep her away from the boredom of looking after her increasingly sedentary and predictable husband.

But Pamela did not want to involve her parents. She needed to make these decisions entirely on her own and, once the initial shock of the pregnancy had subsided, she maintained a steady calm as she ranged over her options – there weren't many.

In a matter of days she had devised a plan. She would do what many a young woman in this predicament had done in generations before her – she would go on a trip for a year or so, maybe 'an educational tour. ' When the child was born it would be adopted and she could return and resume her life.

Pamela delivered her resignation to a startled Ray and Sarah in person so that she could explain that she had decided to withdraw from commercial life and was intent on going away for an extended break to review her future, although she would keep in touch.

She recalled a family holiday in St Ives in Cornwall that she had enjoyed so she contacted a local estate agency which found a small, suitable property for her to rent for up to a year.

Pamela was rather surprised how quickly she was able to engineer a disappearing trick and leave behind her old life and, with just a couple of suitcases, she headed for the West Country to a 'new life'.

She assured her parents that she was just 'taking a break' and that she would keep in touch, as always.

Pamela settled in a tiny two-roomed space on Island Road in St Ives, part of the Island, which was actually a small peninsula between the harbour and Porthmeor Beach. It rose steeply to an outcrop of rock on which was built a tiny chapel.

On the lower reaches around the harbour and the beach on the other side many little cobbled streets of houses gradually spread their sturdy granite walls. Because of the rake of the land, many of the houses opened their front door on one street at first-floor level and their back door at ground level in another.

These spaces at the bottom of the houses were used for decades as the areas where the pilchard catch of the fisherman-owner was processed, stored, salted and distributed.

Here and there among the streets, steps and alleyways that followed the configuration of the landscape, were the smokehouses that also processed the plentiful pilchards, know today as Cornish sardines, since pilchard is a word that, like the fishermen, has gone out of fashion.

Pamela's modest little rooms were just such a space. A cheap kitchen had been constructed on one side of the living room and the bedroom was partitioned off to form a tiny bathroom with shower. Elegant it certainly was not, and there was evidence of damp in both main rooms. But that was the way with these granite cottages.

Above her was a small house that opened out on Burrow Road which, like at least two-thirds of dwellings on the Island, was given over to holiday letting in the season from Easter to September, but mostly July and August.

Where fishermen had all but disappeared, artists remained and St Ives was and remains famous for its artistic community. Painters, potters, writers and musicians all gathered in this most westerly of small English towns, renowned for its Northern light, so beloved of artists.

The intimacy of life was of a different kind to what Pamela had been used to in the Midlands. There was an instant sense of community in St Ives. She came quickly to know the writer who had the little loft place overlooking the harbour, and the tall, brisk elderly gent who strode past her little nest every day with the determination of a man half his years. She came to know him as Bob Crossley, one of the legends of artists who still populated the Porthmeor Studios overlooking one of the beaches. Bob had been a major figure in the art world of the 60os but he dismissed the trappings of the profession and made his own sturdy way, eventually well into his 90s.

Pamela enjoyed the occasional glass of sherry in Bob's home above his shop while he talked of technique and feeling and emotions involved in creating pictures. Then there was the architect who had constructed an awesome wooden house on the very outcrop of rocks of the Island overlooking the harbour one way and the Bristol Channel the other.

She couldn't help but reveal something of herself to the lady in the corner shop and the warm and friendly man in the pasty shop on the High Street who called her "my 'ansome" as he did everyone who frequented his tiny premises. And the weekly visit of the cheery footballer laundryman in his little white van to collect her small bundle of linen was always a highlight.

But being relatively anonymous in the summer bustle of St Ives and the narrow streets around the Island, where Pamela had settled, was one thing. The imminent arrival of a child was quite another. With time to sit and think on the cliffs above the town, staring northwards and eastwards into the Atlantic Ocean morphing into the Bristol Channel, Pamela was able to consolidate her ideas for the future.

After some long sessions on various seats along the cliff-top above St Ives, thinking through what she felt were her options, Pamela decided that she would not return to the Midlands. ,She recognised that amidst the misery of her situation there was an opportunity. She would simply re-invent herself.

Her savings and the pay-off from Sullivan's had left her financially stable for the immediate future, hardly rich but unafraid of routine bills. Maybe she should even change her name?

But whatever she planned for herself, she was resolute that she was too young to be on her own with a child and only vague prospects. This was not a life for a child to be born into and she determined, quite dispassionately, that the child would be adopted to give it the opportunity for a full and settled life without hardship.

Pamela recognised that there was a strong element of selfishness about her decision, which allowed her to pick up the pieces of her own life without hindrance of a child. But she reasoned that the circumstances in which the child had been conceived hardly amounted to a loving relationship that had gone wrong, rather a huge tragedy that had befallen her and which was now reminding her on a daily basis of that terrifying ordeal.

No, it was decided. Pamela took no advice from anyone, indeed she hardly had more than passing contact with anyone, other than her parents, since the idea had been all along to 'disappear' whilst the baby came to term and made its eventual appearance in the world.

The intimacy of life in that old part of town among the granite cottages had enabled Pamela to order her life in a calm and relaxed way. A year of mooching about in St Ives from the desperate cold, wet days of winter trudging through empty cobbled streets, to the almost nauseating crowds of sweating, sauntering 'emmets' packing those same streets in summer, blocking traffic, and inadvertently feeding their pasties and ice creams to the viciously attacking sea-gulls, had determined her to try her luck in the capital city - London.

The need for human contact in St Ives was served by the occasional chat with one of the neighbours a few feet away but isolated by the thick stone walls of the cottages. Norway Stores on Back Road East served most of her domestic supply needs and a comforting word from Mancunian owners Janet and Roy.

She often sneaked back of an evening because a sudden urge for chocolate or Marmite and a cheery banter with Ray, an impossibly gaunt man with a lively London sense of humour, who worked the evenings and days off for the owners.

Their constancy was a comfort in itself, a gentle enquiry as to her circumstances from time to time, but never aggressive intrusion.

In such a setting she organised the adoption of her child. Despite the advice of the agency staff, she opted for an immediate handing over of the child at birth, barring complications.

Pamela was adamant that her child should have a stable, comfortable home with loving parents, able to provide the opportunities that she had no idea whether she would ever be able to do.

And so, after slightly more than the anticipated 38 weeks, Pamela travelled by taxi to Truro hospital some 20 miles away and gave birth to a fine, healthy boy with a tousled mop of black hair. The midwife presented him to her, just as he was, wrapped in blankets. Pamela held him for a few minutes, then said: "OK, take him away, please." It was done.

Chapter thirty-one

Pamela had not long moved from Cornwall to London when the comet Martin Hawes crashed into her little planet. She found an agreeable ground floor flat in a large house In Ealing to rent. It was a new conversion, so was smart and quite decently furnished.

Its best feature was a large, sunny south-facing garden laid to lawn with some flower beds around the perimeter. It felt like a new beginning for Pamela and, although the owner/landlord had more than a touch of 'Rigsby' from 'Rising Damp' about him, she was content.

When he had asked her name, Pamela hesitated, remembering her vow made in Cornwall: "Jenny" she said suddenly, "Jenny Gerber." The discrepancy with her official documents was easily explained away - 'Jenny' was a pet name in the family and it had stuck.

She repeated the name over and over again in the quiet of her bedroom. She had some of the same feelings she had had as a teenager back in dreadful Cranby, daydreaming a little and wondering what life was about to offer her.

This time it was a little different. She had some money but she had a bigger hole in her heart than she cared to admit about the fate of her little baby. She was determined to move on. She had had a lot of experiences in the East Midlands and refused to be scarred by the one horrific event which had pitched her first to the far West Country and then, as if on the rebound, to London, a place she knew only slightly.

Having rented out her house near Belsingham, thus self-sustaining and appreciating as an asset, meant that her furniture was tied up for the remainder of the lease.

But that was OK. Pamela reasoned that it all brought back too many bad memories and she preferred to make a new start

So here she was, in her 20s, sitting in a smart but blandly furnished flat in Ealing, a short walk from the North Ealing Piccadilly Line Underground station which would whisk her into the centre of London in ten minutes or so, like so many young women migrating from the provinces to try and make their fortune in the capital.

But as much as she may have had some income, 'Jenny' still had to have a purpose and make new friends or admit defeat and head back to the East Midlands.

She scoured the jobs columns in the Evening Standard before circling one with a felt-tip pen ' PR assistant required – busy West London agency.'

Having had a dramatic change of hair-style with blonde highlights installed and a series of high-fashion clothes purchases, Jenny sailed through the interview and congratulated herself on her metamorphosis from Cornish village mum-to-be to aspirational girl about town in the metropolis.

Jenny quickly settled into a normal working life and the pain of the previous year, climaxing with the loss of her baby, began to fade. She made new friends at the agency, which was a frenzy of client-pleasing activity. The hours were crazy at times and the boss, Susan Brush, a master, or mistress, of the art of the impossible.

Jenny watched aghast on more than one occasion when Susan pitched to clients and blithely promised them anything and everything they didn't realise they needed for their product – simply to get the business.

Delivering was, of course, an entirely different matter. 'Oh, don't worry about that' was Susan's standard response to the staff to any promise she had made which was beyond the capability of any human being to deliver.

'Darling, of course we will do it. Some silly girl in the office must have forgotten' would be the response to the client over another lavish lunch at the Ritz.

Jenny wasn't comfortable with this kind of 'anything goes' public relations but, since she was an out-of-sight 'junior', she just kept her head down and focused on the social side of her work.

Just for fun she rang for tickets to the recording of a prime-time television comedy show and, within a couple of weeks, she was heading into a television studio in East London with Melanie from the office to watch the recording of "Time After Time".

Melanie was the same age as Jenny, but from Essex, and her idea of a good time was to get as much alcohol as possible down her neck before 'going back to his or mine' with whatever item of masculinity happened to cross her path during the course of the evening.

That, at least, was her idea of 'current affairs,' since opening a newspaper or watching the news on television stretched her attention span too far. Nevertheless she was a happy girl and an active companion – both qualities that suited the vastly more sophisticated Jenny.

And Jenny also valued the generosity of Melanie's friendship – even if it did lead her into some tight corners in bars from time to time.

In the studio both girls gazed in awe at the three not quite full-size sets built around the walls and the rows and rows of numbered lights hanging from the ceiling. Cameras and cables were everywhere.

A rather indifferent comedian came forward through the set and told a series of rather smutty but nevertheless funny stories, which set the audience laughing. Then a slim, tanned man in shirtsleeves, partly rolled up, and black trousers walked on to the set applauding the departing comedian.

"He's pretty fit", hissed Melanie to Jenny who nudged her agreement.

"Ladies and gentlemen, " began the man," my name is Martin Hawes and I am the producer of this programme. So the buck stops right here, " he added, pointing at his own chest.

"In a moment I will introduce the stars of the show, but first I want to ask you to undo your trousers, loosen your bras and have a good time. It's a funny show, so please……..I beg you……think of my wife and children…….for God's sake LAUGH whenever you feel remotely like it. If you don't, I get hauled before the man at television headquarters, and ……………shot ! "

The warmed-up audience laughed and applauded enthusiastically, rising to a pitch of excitement as the stars strode out from behind the set one after another.

Melanie and Jenny clutched each other briefly. "Shame about the wife and kids," muttered Jenny," I could certainly have a laugh with him."

The recording stretched on over several hours and whilst it was not too difficult to keep the laughter going with the frenzied exhortations of the floor manager, sitting on the bone hard seats which had been pulled out of racks against the rear wall of the studio, and watching the leading man continuously forget his lines, was beginning to numb their backsides. A drink would not have gone amiss.

Eventually, nearly three hours after it had begun, the recording of this half-hour episode was declared complete. The audience stood up in relief and began to seek urgent treatment for their stiffness and dehydration in the hot studio.

Melanie and Jenny did likewise and were turning to exit their row when Martin Hawes appeared before them. "Judging from my monitors in the control room, you two seemed to have enjoyed that. Thanks for sitting through it. It was a bit longer than usual. Wouldn't have been so bad if a certain actor had learnt his lines, but there you go. Would you girls like to come to the green room for a drink ?"

His bright smile and smartly understated appearance were instantly appealing and both girls responded with enthusiasm.

Once in the green room, among the assembled actors and actresses, it was clear that Martin was fixing on Jenny. She was modestly surprised, especially as she was still wearing office kit, a straight dark skirt and white shirt unbuttoned one space more than necessary - old 'training' dying hard !

Amidst the hubbub of the room and plenty of 'you were wonderful, darling' comments being lobbed superciliously among the showbiz element, Jenny began to realise that she had really only focused on the deep brown eyes of Martin Hawes.

Somehow she was mesmerised by this man – electrifying smile, gentle almost imperceptible touches and near-hypnotic conversation. Her face settled into a wide smile, teeth apart, her head on one side and one hand involuntarily touching her hair from time to time. No-one else existed, even Melanie, who was in any case busy attaching herself to one of the supporting actors – male.

Martin was 44, had been married and divorced and thus could be considered within polite society to certainly be a catch – but not necessarily for a woman so much younger, no matter how diverse her experience might have been.

Nevertheless the match was made that night in a green room at television headquarters. What became an instant one-night stand became a moving into quite unsuitable but pretty upmarket bachelor flat and a rollercoaster blur of dinners, lunches, parties and a stream of new friends - all in the company of this marvellous man who came to worship her.

Sex with Martin was hilarious – but good. He never seemed to switch off until he fell asleep, and even then he chuntered away in his sleep as though he were solving the problems of the world in another place.

Jenny lay in his makeshift bed in the chaotic flat and grinned silently. She felt elated at meeting this bundle of energy and wit who was clearly beloved by his work colleagues and was a real personality in any gathering. He had pursued her in the studio with a fixation that was flattering and a wit that was beguiling.

She literally laughed her way into his bed – and the fun didn't stop there. By the time he had stopped role-playing various types of heroic lovers from history, Jenny was exhausted, mostly from laughing but also from Martin's skilful attention to her physical and mental condition. He made love as he appeared to live life – at a cracking pace and with an ever-present comic idea.

She recalled the instant attraction she had experienced with Clancy, but that was pure animal lust. He was a powerful man with a fine body and a purposeful way of possessing a woman. With Clancy she felt strong but submissive as she was forced to concede to him, and there was some considerable pleasure in the concession.

Martin teased her into action, into life, like bringing texture to a limp strand of wool or hair. People had to respond to his energy, his positive force. It was inconceivable that such a man could be depressed or withdrawn. Jenny was swept off her feet with the gale force of his personality – and she loved it.

Life became a great adventure. She realised that the Midlands had been fun but a bit of a slog. People there were fundamentally severe, dour even, and looking to make a buck, preferably at someone else's expense. She had joined that pursuit with her artful conversion of her cool looks and serious attraction into a successful business life of her own.

But it had taken the catastrophe of France and the tragedy of bearing a son, whom she had given away, to shatter that existence and force her to profoundly change direction.

How lucky was she to meet a man like Martin within months of setting up in London, she wondered. If there was a God or a guiding spirit for her then He or She had looked after her extremely well. On the other hand, she reasoned, life is about looking at one's circumstances and making decisions according to one's instinct – or inner voice. To that extent we all make our own luck, she decided.

Without in any way accepting what those four men had done to her in Cannes, Jenny was able to take a step back and look at the impact on her life relatively dispassionately. She had decided to bide her time in seeking revenge on the quartet and she had dealt with the immediate issues in a clear-headed way.

That had helped her enormously to deal with the hardships that the attack heaped upon her – the destruction of her way of life, almost of her life itself, had she allowed herself to sink into despair or depression. And her ability to rise above the circumstances and order her future gave her even greater self-confidence than she had already developed by being uninhibited in her close relationships, temporary and longer-term.

Now this mercurial man, an inspired and creative leader and therefore a brilliant producer of television projects, was whisking her to another level of possibilities in the happiest of circumstances.

Chapter thirty-two

Jenny gave herself completely to the relationship with Martin. Mutual attraction has a happy knack of putting together people who have need of the qualities of the other – mostly without realising it. Jenny was beginning to understand how Martin was feeding her self-confidence to realise that she was an attractive, clever, well-informed and skilful communicator.

Her lines of communication lay in making people feel comfortable, relaxed and looked after in her company. She used her skills as a hostess to prepare meals at the drop of a hat and to run a household that was ready for almost any circumstance that Martin might throw at it.

And she carried that cool organisation into work in PR too. Her preparation complemented exactly his spontaneity and energy. Martin stirred people up. He inspired them to work better, harder, longer, faster. He constructed the platform for success out of invisible planks.

He flew, but somehow he always managed to find Jenny's airport. In a matter of months they decided to formalise this partnership and set up their own platform for mutual success.

Paradoxically the wedding was a very low-key affair at Kensington Register Office with maybe a dozen guests. True, several were household names from television, acting, and presenting, and a small crowd gathered outside after the ceremony to greet, not the happy couple, but these several guests.

Standing on the steps of this large converted terraced house, given over to the shabby chic of its official function near a grand Kensington Square just behind the High Street, the little crowd presented few problems for their professional photographer friend, Gill Shaw, to capture the moment.

Half a dozen cars ferried the entire wedding to Notting Hill and the bachelor flat for animated conversation and conspicuous alcoholic consumption for quite some hours, before the principal couple sped off to Heathrow for their honeymoon in Mauritius – organised, needless to say, by Jenny, but Martin made the plane somehow.

In the continuity of conversations between Martin and Jenny leading up to the wedding, she had covered her past pretty comprehensively although still just a little selectively. She had indeed parlayed a minor waitressing job into a career in PR, which had proved very successful in the East Midlands.

She had decided, she told Martin, that the Midlands were a little on the incestuous side with the same old faces doing the same daft things, so she had decided to take a break and re-think her career prospects by spending some time in Cornwall to re-assess her life. Martin was impressed at her ability to stop and take such a cool, hard look at things. He relied on others to shape a direction for him. All his energy went into the moment, the latest idea, the new series

Martin's career took off amidst the exuberance of the relationship. Almost subconsciously he had found the missing piece to the jigsaw of his life. Professional advisers he had plenty, talented staff he marvelled at on a daily basis, but a supportive, stimulating relationship that provided an anchor for his voyages of discovery had been missing. Now she was there.

In this solid state of organisation, one successful television series followed another and his production company was the talk of the industry.

Success brought money in sufficient quantities for the pair to settle into a four-bedroom house in Bedford Park, Chiswick, an almost secret, leafy residential quarter adjacent to the socially-ascendant Chiswick High Road. There was even a heated outdoor swimming pool – something to which even Pamela Gerber had never really aspired !

Jenny busied herself with furnishing the house, having given up full-time PR work, and enjoyed the luxury of a daily swim in the garden in summer. She skilfully combined Martin's few possessions with her own even fewer (having sold her Northamptonshire home complete with furniture) to personalise the otherwise glossy magazine interior – and she set about developing the output of the kitchen for the many friends who tended to pop in on the way out of London to the North and West.

Her natural gift for playing the hostess, and her latent experience gained at Ray and Sarah's parties, soon made Martin's place an invitation to be treasured whether for a small dinner party or open house at the weekend.

Jenny couldn't help but feel lucky. She doubted if anyone could be happier than her. She had put behind her some doubtful and dark experiences and now she had a full and colourful life – a little PR work here, a few lunches mainly with girlfriends and wives of Martin's associates there.

There was no particular point at which Jenny became aware of Martin carrying his relationships a little further than friendly or professional. His hours were erratic to put it mildly but he worked hard and tended to play hard when the occasion permitted.

He often dined out without Jenny ' it's business, darling' but she never felt insecure. Actresses and production assistants came and went, in the house and out. But she did notice that one or two had something of a knowing smile when they came to dinner at their house. Martin was very tactile – it was part of his attraction – and after a while, Jenny could tell which were the fond but professional touches and which lingered a moment or two too long.

Nevertheless she felt secure enough to exercise her flirtatious technique, especially as hostess in her own home. Martin even complimented her on drawing almost passionate endorsements from several of their friends and acquaintances – both male and female. 'Good for business, darling, well done.'

Jenny recalled one particular evening when Martin came home with a disparate group of writers, technicians and actors to continue discussion about his latest project over some food and a flow of wine.

Melanie, Jenny's closest friend was, as ever, putting the world to rights over a bottle or two of red wine with Jenny. Melanie had lost none of her wild child behaviour, apt to attempt anything that took her fancy. Her tales of outrageous behaviour at functions and parties kept Jenny constantly amused when they met for a drink or had lunch together.

She was now well into her thirties, still trim but with some effects of alcohol consumption featuring on her hips and waistline, and ready for anything at any time. Her husband, Ted, a senior executive in public relations, rather delighted in his wayward wife because she always came back to him from whatever adventure she had pursued and told him everything.

He realised that she simply looked for fun and action but that their marriage remained the most important factor in their relationship. Besides, there were the children to consider and they were all-important too.

On this particular evening the production talk was gradually lost in the increasing libation of wine and soon Melanie was leading the proceedings through some of her recent hilarious activities.

She announced to the remaining company – several had drifted off home – that they should all play poker – for forfeits. Everyone thought this an extraordinarily good idea, given an understanding of what the forfeits were likely to be.

Jenny was totally into the idea but was a little unsure, given that there were four men and just herself and Melanie on the female front, of how Martin might react. And the memories of that alcohol-fuelled attack in France stirred uncomfortably in her mind. Inevitably the scene progressed into the shedding of clothes, mostly by the girls, who were soon down to their minuscule pants.

Initially the forfeits for the girls consisted mostly of a little action between the two of them and neither was an unwilling party to that. But soon, most of the guys were all but naked too and their idea of forfeits became a little more personal.

Invited to perform a certain sex act on one of the writers, Jenny raised an eyebrow to Martin as if to seek his affirmation. His confident tilting of his head with both eyebrows raised and a broad smile was sufficient for her to go ahead.

Eventually the group settled into a full-blown orgy with the two women taking on all-comers as alcohol-fuelled lust overcame them all. For Jenny it was good-natured fun and exciting to be back in the swing of things, although she was careful not to demonstrate too much expertise. But she was concerned still at Martin's ultimate reaction, even though he had enthusiastically had sex with Melanie and her in various combinations.

When finally the crowd had sated its collective lust and downed a quick coffee to temper the fading effects of the alcohol, Martin and Jenny retired to bed. "Well, that was a bit of unexpected fun," said Jenny cautiously.

"Darling, you were fantastic. I'm so proud of you. The whole thing just took off, didn't it and I thought you were the sexiest thing on two legs. Come here….." Martin grabbed her and launched into a further session of hectic love-making. OK, so that's alright with him then !

Every year they hosted a grand summer party towards the end of August when most people had come back from the South of France or California – and it was always fancy dress. The costumes became more outrageous by the year and Jenny spent some time on developing hers and Martins before each event. It reminded her of the care with which Sarah organised her events in years gone by.

One year she kitted Martin out in a full chef's outfit including blue check trousers, white jacket and the high hat. He had a tea-towel tucked into his belt and a rather risky–looking knife alongside it. Martin had added a pantomime bushy moustache waxed at each end in the French 'style gastronomique.'

She was Cleopatra, modelled on the Elizabeth Taylor version with heavy black eye make-up and a shimmering green gem-studded dress and head-dress. She looked impossibly beautiful.

The party was possibly the biggest success they had. Many guests got very drunk, some fell in the pool, others had to be rescued by more vigilant partygoers who detected signs of drowning.

It was quite like old times, thought Jenny, except that the canoodling was rather more discreet and few people actually took off all their clothes. A semi-nude 'conga' line snaking around the garden and the ground floor of the house was about as exuberant as this metrosexual crowd became. But Jenny did not fail to notice Martin quietly sauntering off down the garden late in the evening with his arm around a very young man dressed mostly in rags.

"Who was he?" was her casual enquiry the next morning as they lay recuperating in the master bedroom. Various guests were spread among the other rooms having failed to respond to a taxi offer or having had their car keys forcibly removed from their pockets.

"Darling, surely you guessed from his costume! He was Oliver Twist." And there it was left.

Chapter thirty-three

One of Martin's closest advisers was his lawyer Sam Leake. Sam was a constant presence in the background of Martin's life but very much in the foreground of his business. He was the quiet voice in Martin's ear that pointed out some options in the way forward to both realising Martin's quest for creative freedom on the one hand and financial security on the other.

One day he surprised Martin by suggesting to him that it was time to sell his company. It seemed to Martin like the very opposite of what he wanted from life. The company <u>was</u> his life. Planning, organising and completing productions occupied 14 hours of most days. He seemed to have a golden touch with one successful series after another and he had a magnificent bunch of producers working for him to take each series forward year on year.

No, it was time to sell to one of the really big boys in the industry, said Sam, and let them balance the cost against the ongoing world-wide sales and inevitably declining commissions as the series reached the end of their shelf lives around the globe.

But for a conglomerate the opportunity to re-package and re-platform the 'brands' that Martin had established was a world apart from where Martin wanted to be. He was the antithesis of a corporate man.

His 'consigliore' Sam had realised this, a step apart from Martin's hectic schedule as he was, and soon had Martin's agreement to sound out the possibility of a deal.

And some deal it turned out to be. The company remained intact and jobs were safeguarded as Martin became an extremely rich man within a matter of a few years after his marriage to Jenny. But Sam's trump card in the deal was yet to be played………..

After seeing out his service contract with the new owners, Martin simply started again, although he maintained a rather less hectic schedule and sought to develop his interest in powerboats. As with everything about his life, it became a consuming passion and Jenny found herself more than once standing on a windswept marina quay in Cowes or Poole peering through binoculars at a plume of spray behind a dart of a boat racing along the Solent or the Dorset coast, apparently containing her husband.

The smell of fuel and endless engine parts became another fascinating facet of her life.

But nine years into this tumultuous marriage, tragedy struck. Jenny was at home when the call came. Martin was working in the very same studio in East London in which they had met when he collapsed to the floor of the control room.

He was hustled into an ambulance and carried into St Thomas's Hospital on the south bank of the Thames, where Jenny raced in a taxi. But he was dead following a heart attack when she arrived and she sank, shattered, into a chair in the bleak but comfortable Relatives Room, to contemplate life without its driving force.

Despite the close attention of Melanie in particular and their wide circle of friends along with the calm efficiency of Sam Leake in ordering Martin's affairs, it was to be many months before a renewed Jenny began to emerge and fashion a life as a glamorous, wealthy widow.

Chapter thirty-four

Jenny's whole body twitched slightly and involuntarily on her well-padded lounger by the secluded pool at her home in Chiswick. "Pamela," the voice had said – suddenly and unannounced.

She smiled. Her poise was perfect – right shoulder slightly raised, leaning on her left, her breasts hot and exposed in the late morning sun. "Jack Kennedy, I presume ?" she laughed as Jeremy bent to kiss her warmly on the lips. She was pleased to see him.

"Take your clothes off, darling, in the nicest possible way. There's a drink in the fridge."

Jeremy didn't bother with protocol and stripped naked to occupy the lounger alongside her having sprinkled a little pool water on the hot cushions.

Jennifer cast her eye over his firm young body but she restrained those urges. There were more important things to sort out between them.

"Darling, you realise, I suppose, that I'm in love with you." She opened quite deliberately.

"But….."

"Shhhh, let me speak for a moment please."

"I am, shall we say, a wee bit longer in the tooth than you, although I emphasise the 'wee.' But those extra years have taught me a lot and have given me a lot in terms of experience and some understanding of human nature.

"I have been lucky in that life has also endowed me with a great many material things, not least money. So I am in a position to form my own judgements and make my own decisions without reference to other people and without the need to compromise in any way.

" Basically, I don't give a fuck, darling.

"You are an attractive young man but you are still a young man. I like your rather devil-may-care attitude, and your allusions to bi-sexuality conjure up some interesting concepts. I think we could be good together and have lots of fun.

"You will have to run the gauntlet of my friends but once they realise you have my support, they shouldn't cause you too much trouble. But you step out of line with any of the girls – or guys for that matter – and you will be dumped like a ton of horse-shit. Do I make myself clear, sweetie ?"

She took a firm grip on Jeremy's fore-arm to silence him as once again he tried to respond to this gob-smacking monologue. "Now then," continued Jenny smoothly, "apart from the fact that I am probably one of the most desirable women in the Western world, why have you been pursuing me so arduously? And let's have the full truth this time, please.

"If we are going to be together – and I think that we should be – there must be no secrets and no shame between us. So why don't we begin with your full name. I've only ever had Jeremy so far. Where do you come from and what do you do?"

Jeremy could see and feel the determination of Jenny. What he had thought would be a casual visit on a nice, sunny day to push his little investigation a bit further, had been turned on its head and was now a session of truth and consequences.

Not quite the denouement that he had had in mind. He grinned before opening his eyes because this woman had once again outsmarted him and taken the initiative. His mind was reeling because, as she had been speaking, he had felt a rush of real affection for Jenny and realised that maybe this was what love felt like.

The prospect of actually being together as a couple was bouncing around inside his head like a shuttlecock over a badminton net.

Once Jeremy recovered enough mentality to speak, the words began to tumble out. The defences were down, the game essentially was over and it was time for hands to be revealed, cards face up on the table and the pot to be divided.

"My name is Jeremy Leake. My family come from Surrey, but I........." His words were interrupted and drowned by a full-blooded scream from Jenny. "What ? Are you related to Sam Leake, the lawyer ? Tell me he's your uncle. Tell me he's your cousin five times removed, but don't tell me he's your father ! "

"Erm, yes he is."

"Oh my good God. I'm in love with Sam Leake's son. Jesus Christ, how did I get into a mess like this !"

"Hang on a minute, " protested Jeremy. "Things have moved pretty fast for us two and, for sure, I'm pretty attracted to you aside from the need to make my enquiries. But what's wrong with my being Sam Leake's son ?"

"Because he is my lawyer and was my husband's lawyer," gasped Jenny. "I never knew about you. " She quickly calmed down. " But then, why should I have done, and what difference does it make? Surely your father told you about me ?"

"Well, he did and he didn't. Dad's very kosher when it comes to client confidentiality and he would never admit to me that you were a client. No, we only talked in terms of what he knew about my…….er……friend's background, parents and that sort of thing."

Even now he felt the need to be guarded about the identity of his ' client' or 'friend' whose cause he had taken up.

"I recall that I told you in Los Angeles that I meet many different people in many different, and sometimes strange, places. That's part of the nature of the music business. It's not all about young lads and a few girls making a tape and sending it off to the big record company in the sky, hoping for a deal.

"It's about movers and shakers, dealers, chancers, con men, Mafiosi, circus barkers, fraudsters, hucksters, pimps and prostitutes. It's about glamour and glitter, royalty and politics. It's about huge businesses across the globe – big corporations with master plans. And it's about the man who records a hit in his garage.

"That's the landscape in which I move. Someone, somewhere is always looking for a deal, a break or half a chance to show what they can do. Many are certain of their destiny, many others can't see beyond their nose for the next chance or the next pay-day.

"And some," he paused " don't even know where they've come from. This is true of my friend, who wants to know where he came from."

"Oh my God," said Jenny, passion and alarms raised again. "What sort of person is it – oh, he or she ? Do you mean someone who is so off their head they don't know who they are ? Someone who's lost their memory or………….do you mean an orphan or an adopted person ?"

The moment of realisation stabbed through Jenny like the thrust of a stiletto knife, sharp, intense and backed by floods of disconnected possibilities. She began to cry, silently at first, building towards the same great racking sobs which had taken over her body those years before in the South of France. Cries of real, overwhelming, swamping passion.

Jeremy was non-plussed even at the point of uncovering the result of his quest. There was something absolutely bizarre about an almost-naked woman disintegrating before his totally naked eyes. He stuttered for a moment before joining Jenny on her sunbed and wrapping his arms tightly about her.

So much had happened in probably less than half an hour. A little small talk developing into a serious conversation; a declaration of love; and then the naked, disarming reality of a woman in the darkest corners of despair.

Having the warmth and support of a concerned human being enabled Jenny to bring down the level of hysteria until she had reasonably regained some composure.

Realising that their physical appearance was entirely inappropriate to the moment, she gasped: "I must go and get some clothes on."

Jeremy immediately began to organise his own deshabillement and slipped back into his underwear and trousers as he moved into the house to find a drink for Jenny. He felt he knew what was coming but he was still not certain. The only certainty was that it would require a stiff brandy.

In the cool of Jenny's kitchen he found the brandy and a couple of glasses. Within moments she had returned, face freshened and a shirt and pair of shorts covering her nakedness.

"Well, this is turning into a real kiss and tell, isn't it ? " she said with what little dignity she was able to muster. " I don't want you to go on just yet, because I think there's some other things I need to tell you. And maybe, just maybe, we will both arrive in the same place.

"You know all about Sarah's parties and you seem to know a few of the characters I knew particularly well. But I don't think you know what happened that made me leave that scene and what followed.

"You know I got married to Martin and, despite various little dalliances on both sides - and with both sexes it seems, " she added with dark humour, "we were very happy indeed. I had lots of friends, I did a little work, I had my own money and he was loaded after the sale of the business.

"What you probably didn't know was that your father was a genius who managed to insert a clause into the sale of the company which allowed for Martin to be paid again if his company was sold on to another buyer within a certain time period. And it was.

"Poor Martin never saw the money, of course, but it came to me as the residual shareholder or something and left me very comfortable indeed.

"However, the past prior to Martin is the important bit between us. I had a really horrible experience involving several of the regular partygoers from Sarah's. I was seeing Eden James occasionally and he invited me to his house in the South of France one weekend – lovely idea.

"Except that when I got there he was in the house with his wife and a whole bunch of friends and I got stuck in an apartment in Cannes out of the way. I was bloody annoyed to put it mildly. But he has a real roguish charm when he wants to and he smoothed things over.

"The next thing I knew, he came tearing in with his friends and, oh............" Jenny dissolved into tears again between sobs. Jeremy gently pushed the glass of brandy to her lips and she sipped some of the warming and calming liquor.

"Spare me the details," said Jeremy grimly. "I think I know what comes next."

"There was Jamie Avonborough, Isaac Kernow, and Clancy Turner, oh God, it was awful. What could I do? No-one would believe me? I cried and cried and cried. They just left, laughing."

"But surely you took action against them in England," said Jeremy.

"How could I? It would have been my word against theirs and there were four of them ! As far as their wives knew they had just popped down to the village bar for a quick one and they came back with a skinful. Only I was the quick one !"

Jeremy held her tight for several minutes and no words passed between them.

"But, the worst thing was…….." and Jenny began weeping again. "I……I…..I found out that I had become pregnant a few weeks later. And I had no idea which of them was the father?"

"What happened then, to the baby?" asked Jeremy gently.

"I could never have got rid of it, but then neither could I keep it. The only way for me was to disappear for a while, have the baby and then have it adopted at birth before I could get attached to it. So I rented a little place in Cornwall, in St Ives, and lived quietly through the pregnancy."

Jeremy paused for what seemed to him like minutes: " What child did you have?"

"A……boy……." Jenny returned to great, heaving sobs and was inconsolable for many minutes.

Jeremy stayed beside her and cuddled her tightly. God, this was devastating, such a confession from a woman with whom he had just realised he was in love with. What else was coming ?

But could this be ? Was this the answer to Michael's questions ? Had Jeremy succeeded against all odds in tracking down his 'brother's' natural mother ?

Finally he said: " darling, what happened to your little boy."

"I…I….I….don't really know. Oh, I've missed him so much over the years.

Every now and then I would think about him and what had happened to him – whether he was well, was happy, was with a nice family who cared about him. But I knew nothing – and that was the way I wanted it at the time. Just take him away and let the world move on.

"Nobody really told me how hard it would be, not knowing where he had gone, what he was called, who he was with, if they were decent people who would look after him. The adoption people were all very well and 'oohed' and 'aahed' about everything, saying that he had gone to a wonderful family. But that was all that they would tell me because I said I didn't want to know. That was before I realised what bonds are formed between a mother and her child. Do you think this friend of yours could be something to do with me, then?"

"Well," said Jeremy slowly, " he's just turned 25 now so the time frame would seem to fit, and he was adopted as a tiny baby. "

" I must meet him," broke in Jenny. " I must meet him. Do you hear ?" she began to shout and jumped up shaking Jeremy by the arms.

"Okay, okay," said Jeremy soothingly, guessing that this was not the moment to reveal the identity of his 'friend.' "I will arrange a meeting. I think there's a strong possibility that you two might be related."

Chapter thirty-five

Jenny could have been standing before God at the Final Judgement, she was that nervous. She was pacing up and down between her bedroom, the en-suite bathroom and the landing beyond. Her arms were dead and her legs were struggling to maintain enough rigidity to hold her up.

She had moved on from the nakedness of her long soak in the bath to at least wearing some plain white lace underwear beneath her silk robe. Her mind was racing over her entire world as it stood at that moment. The mere fact of what to wear to meet this person who could potentially..........must be.........WAS her son after 25 years.

What if he WASN'T her son ? What if he hated her on sight and shouted at her ? What if he turned out to be some ghastly weed ? What if he attacked her ? All these irrational flashes sped through her mind as she paced recklessly around her house. Oh God, this was the most awful day of her life. She wanted to die, right now and be done with the whole bloody lot of it.

And yet…..it could be the greatest day of her life. A reunion with the baby she had given up in a moment of youthful insensitivity. The making of a family she always felt she had that no man she had loved had given her from among those who had made love to her.

There was still two hours to go before she needed to walk down to Pug, the smart metropolitan brasserie on Chiswick High Road. She blazed at the clock to try and make it go faster. No, she would drive and not walk, it was too hot to walk. No, she should take a cab. Where was that cab number she had hardly ever used.

She dashed down to the kitchen and checked her notice board. Plumbers, electricians, flower shops and the local Indian takeaway all had a spot – but no cab number. It must be in a handbag somewhere – but which handbag?

She ran back up the stairs two at a time. Finally, she sank back on to her bed and disintegrated into tears. She needed help to organise herself. She, Jenny Hawes, the great organiser, the leading socialite, the hostess no-one turned down, needed help from almost anyone just to put herself together and calm down enough to meet this young man - her son ?
She rang Melanie.

Chapter thirty-six

Jeremy moved nervously up and down the long bar inside Pug. It was barely after 12 mid-day and he checked and re-checked the details of the lunch in his mind. It was a familiar routine in some respects because he was used to checking such fine detail for the receptions and parties he was paid to organise in his music industry role.

But this was different – this was personal. And he was right on the edge. He walked up and down, occasionally picking up his Kir Royale and putting it back down again. Should he have a bottle of champagne at the table or should he wait to see how the meeting went prior to the arranged lunch?

What if they weren't what he thought they were? What if they hated each other on sight? What if there was a screaming match? It could all go horribly wrong. Jesus, he wished he had never got into all this for Michael.

Pug is set back from Chiswick High Road with a large square courtyard which is filled in summer with extra tables and the chance to bask in the mid-day sun over scrambled eggs and smoked salmon with a chilled Pinot Grigio perhaps.

Entering from the High Road there is a long room to the left of the yard with cubicles and leather banquettes. That and the main doors lead into the long bar with a comfortable reception area to the right. Beyond all this is the restaurant proper with the kitchens off.

Jeremy had fixed to have the last but one cubicle from the High Road, and arranged, with a significant compensation to the maitre d', for the ones on either side to remain empty. This enabled him to settle Michael in a seat with his back to the main door and for himself to see Jenny arrive before she could spot him.

If Michael was nervous he concealed it well. He had arrived exactly at 12.15 p.m. as requested, by taxi, with an understanding in the office that he was sounding out a major interview and might not be back.

Few words passed between the two brothers, in their respective seats on the banquettes, as Jeremy restlessly watched each arrival. He got up several times and strolled to the bar area, apparently because of nerves, but actually because he didn't want Michael to notice which person he might be going to greet – or not.

He needn't have worried. Michael had told him when he arrived that he was looking forward to meeting this lady in much the same way as he anticipated a major interview. The difference this time was that he had been unable to do much detailed research and had to rely on what Jeremy had told him in the previous few weeks and – it was personal. That made him, he said, a little uneasy, but he had a way of taking things as they came and it had served him well in his journalistic career to date.

Jenny was under strict instructions to arrive at 12.30p.m. Even in the relatively short time that he had known her Jeremy had come to understand that she operated largely on Jenny-time which rarely bore much resemblance to reality – much like her life.

He was struck how she managed her life with remarkably little intellectual input. She rarely read a book and a flick through a magazine or newspaper was her own particular nod to current affairs and style.

And yet she was patently very intelligent and very much up-to-speed with the goings-on in the world. Somehow snippets of information caught in her web of awareness and she held her own at dinner-table discussions on a wide range of subjects – part of her eternal fascination and finesse as a hostess.

It seemed that life was to be lived very much on her terms with her carefully-filed mental index of friends, acquaintances and people-to-get-to-know. Just as his mind was assessing these thoughts, she arrived.

Jeremy missed her advance across the courtyard but he caught a rear view of her bearing down on the maitre d' at his station between the bar and the restaurant. She had ultimately chosen a black, linen tailored suit having dismissed the notion she herself had raised that it might seem a tad gloomy for such a potentially positive event.

"Hang on here," squawked Jeremy, immediately betraying his anxiety to Michael and the fact that Jenny Hawes had arrived and was, indeed, in the building.

Michael decided against turning around after Jeremy had left the cubicle. Suddenly his stomach had tightened and he was feeling, well, almost faint. That famous cool had dissolved at the prospect of meeting his birth mother.

"Michael," said Jeremy at his brother's left shoulder, "this is Jennifer Hawes."

Michael stood up, his lean, dark frame resembling a sportsman and his short, curly hair the very opposite of his brother's bulky light thatch.

Jennifer pursed her lips slightly, she was trembling, mostly inside, and she looked hard at this attractive young man before her. Instantly there was no doubt in her mind. He was her son.

They made as if to shake hands, then to kiss on the cheek but they did neither. They fell into each others arms and Jennifer wailed: "Oh my God, you are my son!"

Jeremy's careful planning had allowed for this moment as both dissolved into tears and he signalled to the bar, mouthing the word 'champagne.'

There was no interrupting the torrent of words between mother and son. How on earth had she not realised that Sam Leake's son could have been hers ? "Probably because you didn't know I was adopted," Michael hesitated and stopped before the word 'mum' could escape his lips.

But Sam had never said anything and he was Martin's lawyer all those years. "Perhaps he never knew who my parents were ?" countered Michael.

And, of course, Sam had only ever known her as Jennifer, the wife of his television producer client and had never been aware of her earlier life as Pamela Gerber in the Midlands, the parties, the attack, the pregnancy and the assumption of a new identity.

"In fact he only told me within the past year that I was adopted at all, because I had begun to feel so different from the rest of the family and Jeremy in particular. It doesn't take a biologist to observe that Jeremy and I are very different people – much as we may care for one another.

"We have Jeremy to thank for this " said Michael as the champagne was uncorked and flowed into three flutes at the table.

"The toast is – to mother and son," said Jeremy beaming at the obvious success of his mission.

"Thanks, Jerry," said Michael with quietly intense feeling. "While I sat and angsted about all this you got on and made the search and it's quite astonishing that you have succeeded."

Jennifer sat in awe of the fact that suddenly she was in love all over again – with two brothers, one as a son and one as a lover and it was all perfectly legal. A rush of elation burst within her as she grasped a hand of each and said: " boy, have we got some talking to do !"

The trio finally left Pug around 7.30p.m. buoyed by three bottles of champagne and infused with adrenaline and elation at their re-unification after so many years.

The whole conversation was swamped in a whirlwind of catching up with Jennifer carefully editing her contributions despite the loosening effects of the champagne.

The threesome finally broke up with Michael's departure from the house in Bedford Park around 3a.m.

Chapter thirty-seven

"Well, I'll be damned," said Sam Leake softly but firmly. He was seated at his dining table immediately opposite his late client's widow, Jennifer Hawes, looking cool and elegant as ever.

Michael had reported his discovery to his 'father' later in the day after meeting Jennifer and sitting up half the night talking. Sam and Lucy Leake immediately invited her to dinner to discuss this bizarre turn of events.

Jennifer, with interjections from Jeremy and Michael, had relayed those parts of her history of which Sam and Lucy had been unaware, prior to her marriage to Martin, and the story of her attack and the subsequent birth of a son who had been adopted at birth.

"This is not so much a moment that Lucy and I have feared," said Sam, "rather we welcome the fact that Michael appears to have been able, with Jerry's help, to find what he has been looking for, increasingly anxiously, these past months.

"We feel confident that Michael has had a loving environment in which to grow up and I hope that he will continue to look upon us as his parents – surrogate or otherwise. " Michael nodded emphatically and went to hug Lucy and then Sam.

"The circumstantial evidence is pretty compelling," he continued, " but clearly you must each take a DNA test to absolutely confirm what appears to be the case.

"Then I guess, Michael, you will want to pin down who your natural father is.

"At least the field is much narrower for that ! But you will need to tread very carefully. All four of these men have a distinct public profile, to a greater or lesser extent, and you must be scientifically certain of your facts before you give them the slightest hint of what you suspect.

"I urge all three of you to think deeply about what you do next. The circumstances as Jennifer has described of the conception are difficult, not to mention criminal, in either France or England, so you can expect a strong reaction from all quarters if you are anything less than extremely cautious.

"I will help in a professional capacity as much as I can. Now let's go to the living room and have a brandy!"

Michael, Jeremy and Jennifer were seldom apart from then on. They discussed endlessly how to approach the four potential fathers who took part in the assault on 'Pamela' in the South of France.

Every so often one or other discussed their ideas with Sam who either encouraged or discouraged according to the risk factor in each case. Eventually the trio settled on the device of using Michael's column 'Discovering People' to gain access to each individual without their knowing the background or true intention of the process.

Isaac Kernow was flattered to get Michael's call. His assiduous networking and string-pulling through the years had taken him from councillor to leader of Leicester City Council and on to Member of Parliament for one of the city's constituencies.

Gifted with a machiavellian talent for playing one person off against another and scratching as many backs as he felt necessary to advance, he had at first been a model new Member, responding eagerly to the instructions of the Whips and always ready to offer an easy question for Ministers to make their views known at Questions.

Such apparently submissive and pleasing behaviour had got him noticed in the party's upper echelons and he soon found himself on the fringes of a Cabinet post, being a junior minister in the Department of Culture, Media and Sport.

None of the three main areas of the department's work had any particular appeal to Isaac, who's abiding passion continued to be the opposite sex. But he managed to look busy on departmental matters and to keep his other affairs relatively discreet and certainly no more public than many other MPs.

He had special responsibility for supervising the distribution of Lottery funding for the so-called Good Causes or activities that the Government no longer cared to fund from general taxation. This gave him a sense of status and he made the most of whatever power and influence he was able to exert.

Michael Leake played cleverly on Isaac's sense of self-importance as a man to watch in the political spectrum and he really wanted to feature him first, to introduce him to a wider public.

Nothing could have been more calculated to appeal to Isaac's vanity when, if truth be told, he was the very epitome of how an MP had once cynically been defined – an attention-seeker of no discernible talent.

He invited Michael for drinks on the Terrace at the House of Commons, implying that he was such an important and busy person that he could hardly be expected to travel for a mere press interview, but in reality affording him the opportunity to show his parliamentary colleagues that he was to be profiled in a major national newspaper.

Michael began the interview with a few innocuous enquiries about his current range of duties as a junior minister, always couching the questions in the context that Isaac was a man on the move and a coming figure in the world of politics.

Then he threw in the curveball: " Isaac, do you still go to parties ?"

Isaac stumbled verbally and then gathered himself. He was too fly to react instantly to a question like that. First his trademark smile: " Of course. I love to be invited to parties. You meet so many interesting people, and of course it's essential for an MP to stay in touch with the world around him – or her.

"We get so closeted here in Westminster."

"Yes, of course. But when you were leader of Leicester City Council, did you not have something of a reputation for being a party animal ?"

The smile closed to a less radiant, tighter-lipped look and the head began to shake from side to side. "Oh no, I don't think so. Anyway, I thought we were talking about my role at the DCMS.

"But I understand that there was a bit of a controversy over your departure from the Council job. Was that connected to people you associated with in the area ?"

Isaac was becoming agitated and the smile had faded altogether. "Absolutely not," he snapped. "I resigned from the council because I wanted to prepare as a Labour candidate for MP."

"I rather thought you were invited to leave because of a suspicion of favours and benefits between you and some of the people you were close to. Wasn't there a question of planning permission for a company associated with Bechtel, the American corporation ?"

"Look, where the hell are you digging all this stuff up from ? I don't know what you are talking about." Isaac was practically hissing, trying on the one hand to express his anger and wishing on the other that he had not been surrounded by Parliamentary colleagues, not to mention one or two other media people.

Michael persisted, quietly but firmly. "But it was well known that you were friendly with Clancy Turner who was an attorney for Bechtel. What was the strength of that ? Did you not go to parties at Ray and Sarah Barnes together?"

"Look, I've had enough of this, young man. You need to learn a bit of respect for Government ministers instead of muck-raking 20 or 30 years in the past. I was a very successful leader of Leicester City Council. I resigned to prepare for the general election in 1983.

"As leader of the council I met hundreds, if not thousands of people, on council business and socially connected with the council. I can't be expected to remember every function I went to. Now, if you persist in this line of questioning, I will get up and leave and close this interview."

"Oh don't do that, Isaac, because there's someone I'd like you to meet." Michael rose swiftly and stepped back inside the restaurant from the terrace and signalled to Jennifer, who was sitting quietly sipping a glass of wine in the corner.

Jennifer mustered all her regal elegance and stepped on to the terrace. Isaac jumped to his feet in shock, the colour draining from his face. He became so pale and agitated that, for a moment, Michael and Jennifer thought he might have a cardiac arrest.

"Isaac, fancy seeing you again after all these years," said Jennifer at a steady pace. "You haven't changed much, I hear. Still toadying round every woman you can get your hands near?" Jennifer was not speaking particularly loudly, but Isaac squirmed and cowered as if he was being pelted with rotten eggs, desperately hoping that those at the nearby table could not hear her. They could. And conversation in the vicinity of Isaac's table paused as others took in the scene.

Michael rescued the situation with: "Presumably you remember Pamela – Pamela Gerber?"

"Yes, yes, of course," whispered Isaac. "What is all this about ? Why have you brought this lady to the interview ? You're setting me up for something. Let me tell you, young man, that I am well acquainted with the laws of libel."

Turning to Jennifer, Isaac's management systems had restored some calm to his troubled persona, and he smiled – his beaming ingratiating smile. "How are you, my dear? It's marvellous to see you again. You look absolutely fantastic. What on earth brings you to this place ?"

"I can answer that one, Isaac," said Michael. "I gather you two knew each other a few years ago, so I thought you might like to say 'hello' again.

"Pamela, or Jennifer as she has been known for a good many years, is my mother."

He watched as Isaac struggled with his emotions. For once in his life he was completely on the back foot, had no idea really what to do next and yet was aware of the enormous pressure of his surroundings. The last thing he needed was a row on the Terrace about some lark in the South of France 20 years before. He had to escape.

"Well, of course, it's been lovely to have that opportunity. I'm sorry it's going to have to be short and sweet though, Pam…..er……Jennifer, duty calls. I have urgent business to attend to."

"Of course, Isaac," said Jennifer soothingly. She was loving every second of his discomfort. It was nowhere near to re-paying the harm he had done to her but it was certainly very cold revenge. Having seen him again at close quarters with his irregular teeth and that greasy hair combed over his baldness, she just hoped fervently that Isaac was not Michael's father. It would be too much to bear.

Isaac was already on his feet and moving away as he half-turned to Michael and nodded dismissively. "You'd better be very, very careful with what you write. I will have my lawyers go over it with a fine toothcomb, boy."

With that he darted through the doors back into the comforting womb of the Houses of Parliament. Any number of onlookers watched bemused at the whole scene as Jennifer and Michael dissolved into laughter. Eventually they, too, stood up to leave, but not before Jennifer had deftly rolled Isaac's tumbler into her handbag.

Chapter thirty-eight

"Who's next?" laughed Jeremy as Jennifer finished recounting the events of the day. They were wrapped in the fine cotton sheets of the principal bed at her house, television relaying constant news in the background.

"I don't know," said Jennifer. " But I will get the tumbler over to Sam's office in the morning and he can start the DNA process. Now we've got Michael's DNA it's only going to be a process of elimination, isn't it !"

"But we still don't know for absolute certain that you are Michael's mother," cautioned Jeremy. "Let's not get ahead of ourselves."

"I know," said Jennifer, suddenly less light-hearted than she had been. " But I'm expecting to get the results tomorrow at Sam's office."

"In the meantime, then……….." Jeremy reached across and took Jennifer into his arms.

"Oh, you are <u>very</u> naughty," murmured Jennifer without a trace of admonishment in her voice. She turned and moved towards him in the big bed.

As Jeremy snored gently beside her, Jennifer lay quite awake thinking back over the day's events. She had not considered attending the interview until Michael suggested it as being a way of reinforcing Isaac's discomfort and increasing the pleasure of her revenge.

She smiled at the scenes on the Terrace, but the whole episode had really only served to bring back the events of the terrible evening in Cannes. She recalled all too vividly Isaac's leering face that night, Jamie's eyes popping as if caught in the school tuck shop, and Clancy staring at her with a frightening intensity as he clearly enjoyed the moment.

Tears coursed across her cheeks in the dark as she felt again the blows to her mind, body and spirit as the quartet ravaged her body in every conceivable way. It had been so horrible – and yet amongst all this tragedy she had found new love and, most important of all, she had re-discovered her long-lost and much-missed son.

But who had committed the ultimate violation ? Surely not Isaac, that mean-spirited, cunning, calculating man with barely a charitable bone in his body. That he might be Michael's father was too much to bear.

Chapter thirty-nine

"Well, here's to a happy ending !" Sam stood and passed a glass of champagne across his desk to Jennifer, who was wriggling and giggling in her excitement at learning definitively that Michael was her natural son.

"I should caution you, though, that there is a one in many millions chance that he is actually not your son." They both laughed strongly and in a totally relaxed manner.

"Oh, I must call Michael," said Jennifer.

"Begging your pardon," interrupted Sam, "I've already done that. He's on his way over. I guess it was probably the last privilege I might have as his father – of sorts."

"Sam, you will always be Michael's real father, no matter who turns out to have fulfilled the biological deed. I wouldn't want any of them to be regarded as his father after what they did to me. You have done such a wonderful job with him – and so has Lucy – we will forever be in your debt.

"I don't know what Michael's attitude will be towards his natural father when he eventually finds out, as he surely will with these DNA tests. But he's a grown man now, thanks to you, and already a success in his chosen career, so it's up to him how he handles it.

"Oh Sam, I can't tell you how fabulous I feel ! One of the most horrible moments of my life has led to this glorious day. I'm in love with two brothers – and one is my son !

"Oh my God, I shouldn't have said that ! I'm so sorry, Sam. I didn't mean to blurt that out about Jeremy."

"Oh, don't worry, Jenny, Jerry is a grown man too, and it is his prerogative to be in love with whoever he likes. You know, we parents," he winked mischievously, "have to let go of the kids sometime and allow them to make their own choices.

"Jerry has moved around his circle like a butterfly and sometimes I wondered what sort of flower he might alight on. All I can say is I'm glad it's you and I hope you bring each other a lot of happiness. Who knows these days ? Anything goes, it seems and us old'uns have got to stay open-minded. As long as they're safe and well and happy......."

Jennifer jumped up and hugged Sam, just as Michael came striding through the door and joined in the communal hug. "Isn't this great !" he said and kissed his mother many times.

Chapter forty

Michael was sitting on the corner of his desk, telling his assistant the good news when his telephone rang.

"Michael, it's Isaac Kernow. I just called to say thank you for the piece. It's very nice indeed. You surprise me, you young Turk. I thought you were going to stitch me up. But 'Isaac Kernow – The Coming Man,' I couldn't have done better myself."

"Well, Isaac, you are renowned for your powers of discretion, so I thought I would show you that two can play that game. What I put into print and what I know can be two very different things. And what I know, of course, can be dangerous……….. for an aspiring Cabinet Minister – n'est-ce pas ?

"I have a small confession to make, Isaac. I sort of borrowed a tumbler from our table – your tumbler – so the House may be a glass short for a few days. But I will send it back soon, before you send the Serjeant-at-Arms or Black Rod after me."

"What did you do that for?"

"Ever heard of DNA, Isaac?"

Isaac screamed: "You bastard !" and slammed down the phone.

Chapter forty-one

Jeremy and Michael were seated by the door in the bar at Morton's when they heard a familiar voice. "Darling I've been coming here for absolutely a-g-e-s ! What do you mean, <u>member</u>? Don't you recall when I told you the place was on fire that Christmas Eve ? Saved you thousands in repairs.

"Oh, there you are Michael, please tell this lovely man that I have been a member of this place for centuries." Michael pressed a small folding note of the realm in the receptionist's hand as Jennifer swept into the bar, sunglasses blazing.

The trio found a cubicle by the window, and went into session. Michael reported his conversation with Isaac, much to the amusement of all and they debated the next move in the 'Grand Quest' to discover Michael's father.

"We should know in a few days about Isaac," said Jeremy.

"No, let him sweat for as long as possible," countered Jenny. "I've thought long and hard about this. Let them all sweat once they know the possibility. After the way they treated me they can all go through the same fear and dread that I experienced all those years ago. At least <u>I</u> had the most marvellously happy ending, darling." She patted Michael's hand. A huge smile was never far from her lips these days.

Jennifer was having enormous fun and revelled in being the centre of attention among her girl-friends who hung on her every word. Every day Melanie pressed her for the latest developments and Jennifer delighted in drawing out the suspense, now that her vengeance was rapidly being consummated.

"No, my darlings, I have asked Sam to keep the DNA results in a safe unopened until we have all of them in hand. It's our task now to obtain samples from the other three. And, as Sam said, we must be very careful and very sure before we say anything to anyone.

"Now Michael, here is the direct number of Eden's p.a. I believe he still has the same woman after 25 years or so, which must be some sort of record for him. God, I bet her story is worth a few thousand from the News of the Screws.

"I am led to believe that he is in the South of France – how apposite ! Perhaps you and Jerry could go together for this interview ! I couldn't bear to go there, ever again. Apparently he doesn't go to the office much these days – he's too idle and too rich."

Nevertheless, of all of them, Jennifer still felt a knot of despair about Eden

James. He was a rough diamond, to be sure, but she had had so much fun with him. He didn't care who thought what about him really and he was a moth to the flame in the limelight.

Next to Clancy Turner, Eden had been her favourite and had remained constant until that unsavoury day in Cannes. Even then he had tried to contact her many times before she finally changed her telephone numbers.

Chapter forty-two

"You must be Eden James," said Michael with outstretched hand in the assembly area outside Nice airport Arrivals.

"Yes, young man. And who is this with you – the photographer ?" said James, clad as ever in Bermuda shorts, loud shirt and large, dark sunglasses – low-key to the last.

"No, actually it's my brother Jeremy, who fancied a trip to the Sud de Frog. He's a whiz at tape-recorders and things like that so I brought him along as a sort of technician, if you don't mind. I wouldn't want to come all this way to find my recorder doesn't work or the batteries have run out or something."

"Nah, no problem, except one of you is going to have to squeeze in the back of the motor" said Eden gesturing towards the bright red Ferrari 356 parked just inside the car park. "Lucky I've got the lid off !" Age may have matured some aspects of Eden's character but the finesse levels remained disturbingly low.

Jeremy opted for the windy seat as he was that much smaller than Michael – a fact already noted by Eden James. "You two are like chalk and bleedin' cheese – are you sure you're brothers ?" He didn't become one of the top ad men in the world by missing the obvious.

The Ferrari sped along the autoroute out of the airport and growled its way around the back roads into the hills and on to the rather ostentatious villa that Eden had built in the earliest days of his brilliant career. He always boasted that if times became hard he could peel off all the gold leaf and cause a blip in the gilt markets.

Soon they were settled in swimming shorts around the pool in sun loungers. Michael's recorder was carefully positioned under the sun-shade on the table nearest to Eden's chair. Jeremy felt quite at home in a situation he had experienced many times before in various hot-spots around the world.

"I can see from the car and the house here, Eden, that you are a man of a certain style, and yet your reputation in the world of advertising is that of someone in touch with the man on the street, comfortable with his lingua franca. How else could you have created so many amazing campaigns for blue-chip brands. ?"

Eden almost purred with contentment. This boy knew how to flatter an old chap. " Well, I've never forgotten my roots, you know. We was dirt poor in them days and I didn't always have shoes to run around in................." Jeremy mentally switched off as James droned on in this fantasy world of his up-bringing.

This was certainly not the first major feature interview he had done and his raconteur skills were nearly as finely tuned as his racketeering ones. He had been a little surprised when the long-suffering Meg had put the proposition to him after Michael's call to her. He hadn't actually been bothered by the media for some years.

He never personally used the word retirement because he still had so many little businesses and deals to run and he tended to be on the phone constantly to one part of the world or another. But he hadn't dreamt up an ad campaign in donkey's years. He wondered what the famous Michael Peake could want with him? He had to find out. None of his associates in London had anything on Peake, so he assumed it must be quite straightforward, a nice piece in one of the rags and problem solved.

Michael patiently allowed James to spiel his story with very few interruptions beyond the odd "really ?" or "goodness me."

"Well, Eden that's all very impressive," he said finally. " I get a very good impression of how you have managed to come up with some of the most memorable tag lines in advertising history.

"But actually you grew up in the Midlands, didn't you? This whole London thing came a bit later. I believe that you even had a business there to begin with. Didn't you do some sort of reverse take-over for the agency that you head up these days ? Or are my researchers wide of the mark ?"

Eden looked at him hard through his impenetrable sunglasses, which prevented the glare from reaching Michael.

"You do do your homework, don't you sunshine," he replied carefully. It had been very many years since anyone had mentioned Leicester in his presence. He lit his seventh cigarette of the interview, slowly took a drag and exhaled the smoke in rings.

"Yes, I had a little business up there for a while. You could call it my apprenticeship, " he laughed stiffly.

"Well, you must have been something of a sorcerer's apprentice from what I gather, " said Michael steadily. " Lots of people up there still remember you. You were very much part of the crowd, by all accounts.'

Eden studied Michael closely. He was concerned at what was coming next. He didn't know what was coming next and he didn't like being in that position of not knowing. His business thrived on him outguessing anyone and everyone. But he had played poker for too many years and for too much money to give away the slightest hint that he was worried.

"What crowd would that be, Michael ?" he said evenly.

"You were, apparently, the life and soul of the party at Ray and Sarah Barnes' house on more than one occasion. I gather their do's were a bit wild even for the swinging seventies."

"Oh, bloody hell," chuckled Eden. "I've always enjoyed a good party and, of course, you meet the most interesting people at affairs like that. They used to invite the best fun people in the region and I won a lot of business by being a prat at their parties. No harm in that, old son.

"No," replied Michael quickly, "but there were a lot of stories at the time of various favours being bestowed on people such as yourself by people like Isaac Kernow of Leicester City Council, for example. Did you know Isaac?"

"Know him? I organised his kid's bar-mitzvah," laughed Eden." Everyone knew Isaac and people like me had to know him if we were to get any business at all. Yeah, there was a bit of scratching of backs but no funny business."

"That isn't quite how 'Private Eye' saw it. And Isaac eventually resigned under a bit of a cloud didn't he ? "

"Look, my little mucker," growled Eden, " You obviously don't know nothing about business life - do you want a nice personality piece about Eden James, adman extraordinaire, or are you poking your nose into places you're not really welcome, if you get my drift."

"Hmmm, scratching of backs," mused Michael out loud. "Did one of those backs belong to Pamela Gerber, by any chance ? You remember Pamela don't you, Eden ?"

"Who? " said Eden, recognising that, at last, the bombshell had arrived. He remained outwardly calm, although his anger was slowly rising. This was territory he never expected a young punk newspaper writer to be treading.

"Pamela Gerber. She was one of the girls who worked for Ray and Sarah at their parties. Didn't you have a bit of a scene with her ?"

"Look, keep it down, lad. There's certain things we boys don't want the girls to hear, do we ?" Eden adopted the laddish approach to deal with this one. "Yeah, and this is strictly off the record and not for printing in your illustrious newspaper, I've had a few little adventures in my time. But who hasn't ? I wouldn't say I outranked Casanova but I've done OK – and I'm still married after 36 years so don't you dare put that in jeopardy or I'll string you up."

"Were you thinking about your marriage when you put Pamela up in your apartment in Cannes 26 years ago? You were in France with your wife and some friends, weren't you? And didn't you and the boys pay her a visit? " Michael added coldly.

"Right. I've heard enough. What's it to do with you. You're just a bleeding nosy parker. You've got enough for a feature, now get out !."

Jeremy could see that Michael was becoming angry and emotional – quite out of character – so for the first time in the interview, he interjected as he grabbed the recorder off the table, before Eden could throw it in the pool.

"Michael is my brother Mr James, but he is my adopted brother. He was born 25 years ago – to Pamela Gerber."

His words drifted after Eden James as he stormed back into his house slamming doors as he went and yelling at his staff: "Get rid of those two fucking nonces."

Michael and Jeremy needed no persuasion to slip on their clothes and head out the front door. Once outside they looked at each other and started to walk down the driveway and off towards the village in search of a taxi.

"Oh bugger," said Michael. "I lost the plot a bit in there and forgot to grab his glass."

"Fear not, brother of mine, " laughed Jeremy. He dipped into the pocket of his swimming shorts inside his outer shorts and pulled out four cigarette butts. "One of these should do the trick !"

Chapter forty-three

The knock on Jennifer's door was confident rather than tentative and yet struck her as not being one of her friends. She was wondering why she felt that as she opened the door.

Two dark-suited men stood there and almost immediately began to move towards her. "Mrs Jennifer Hawes ? We're from I.S.," the leading man said flashing some form of I.D. card towards her as he stepped inside the door, closely followed by his colleague.

Neither smiled as Jennifer protested: "I what ? Who said you could come forcing your way into my home ? What is going on ?"

"I.S. madam, Inland Security. We were established by the recent anti-terrorism legislation and we would like to ask you a few questions," said the first grey man.

"Inland Security ? Questions ? I'm going to call the police ?" said Jennifer still quite startled by the smooth, expressionless way in which the men communicated.

" I wouldn't bother, ma'am. They do as we tell them," said grey man one. Nevertheless, Jennifer dialled 999 and called the police to come and deal with these intruders.

The two men didn't even shrug at Jennifer's action. "Well, we'll take a look around while the plod make their way here," said grey man two.

Despite her fierce protests, the men pushed her aside and strode up the stairs in total confidence. They proceeded to move quickly from room to room, glancing in drawers, running their hands through others and stopping only when they reached Jennifer's computer in her study.

"We'll be taking this, Mrs Hawes, to have a little look inside," said grey man two, unplugging the lap-top and picking it up with its power cable.

Just then a police car scrambled to a halt outside, blue lights blazing and a young constable ran to the door and began knocking. Grey man one unhurriedly went down stairs in front of Jennifer and opened the door. Once again he flashed his I.D. card at the constable and said: "Leave this one to us, sonny," before closing the door, leaving the hatless and hapless constable to walk back to his car, reaching for his shouldered personal radio.

"Now then, madam," he turned to Jennifer with renewed confidence and authority, "shall we have that little chat ?"

The group took seats in her living room, beige and white throughout apart from a couple of brilliantly-coloured Bob Crossley paintings paired on one wall and some etchings framed on other walls.

"We understand that you had a little run-in with a member of the Government recently, Mrs Hawes, with your son who is quite a well-known journalist, I believe."

Jennifer faltered, still in shock at the presence of these two cold, grey men, and now surprised at the apparent reason for their visit. She was shaking slightly, a fact not unnoticed by the two men who looked at each other and almost smiled.

"I had a very brief encounter with Isaac Kernow on the Terrace at the House of Commons the other day," said Jennifer," but I would hardly call it a run-in. I had scarcely said 'hello' and he ran off like a frightened rabbit."

"Perhaps, madam, that was because of the threat you and your son made to him."

"Certainly not, don't talk nonsense......."

"We never talk nonsense, madam. Terrorism comes in many forms these days and it may have escaped your notice that to demonstrate within one mile of the House of Commons, let alone inside it, is a criminal offence."

Brushing aside Jennifer's incredulous protests, he continued: " we take any form of terrorism, threatened, conspired, discussed or even implied, extremely seriously. I could have you locked up without a key inside the hour if I so chose.

"Now, this is what we would call a friendly visit to just mark your card as it were. Threatening a Government minister is not on and the Government doesn't like it – one little bit. Nor does our department.

"So tell sonny Jim, the pen-pusher, to be a little more careful about what he writes and what he says to Parliamentary figures on the Government benches or the next visit won't be half so friendly. Alright, dear ?"

With that the two men stood in unison, turned with her lap-top and exited the room and the house as smoothly as they had entered it. Jennifer went to the window and saw them climb into a nondescript black saloon car and drive away with hardly an intrusion into the traffic.

She sat down sharply on the plush sofa and held her hands to her face. She was shaking. The men had been so cold, so matter-of-fact, she wondered what sort of training school turned out ghastly human beings like that.

How on earth could a harmless newspaper interview involve the security services – especially one of which no-one had heard. Just how paranoid was this government ? Had 1984 finally arrived ? Twenty years late maybe, but terrifying all the same.

Michael exploded uncharacteristically into apoplexy when Jennifer finally reached him on the phone. "Don't do anything, Michael," pleaded Jennifer as fear replaced her anxiety. "They were real, and very frightening."

Even Sam was perplexed by the visit. "There was nothing in the piece that reflected badly on Kernow. What on earth caused the spooks to wake up?" He, too, was unaware of this Inland Security department but the briefest of checks with his contacts confirmed that it did, indeed, exist.

The feature in Michael's newspaper had said nothing detrimental about Isaac Kernow but had rather confirmed him, as promised, as an emerging figure in politics, destined possibly for Cabinet status soon.

"It must have been the conversation I had with him afterwards," said Michael to his mother when he arrived at her house to find her nursing a large brandy.

"I told him that we had taken the glass from the table and that we were going to have it DNA tested to try and establish who my father is. He wasn't at all amused and clearly has used what political muscle he has within the party. After all, even in this government, a scandal like this would certainly halt his career and end any chance he may have of getting into the Cabinet."

"Oh God," said Jennifer, "and he's only the first. What will the others try ?"

Chapter forty-four

Jennifer stepped from the cab and swept into Le Caprice. She was greeted like the old friend she was and shown to her usual table – number seven – when some author or other hadn't grabbed it first.

There sat Melanie, her dearest and closest friend, who had lived through the whole second phase of her life and who had gradually become the sole custodian of all of Jennifer's secrets.

Melanie had mellowed a great deal from her early Essex bingeing days, collared herself a captain of the PR industry who doted on her dottiness, and these days she restricted herself to red wine – quite a lot of red wine - but unmixed with the mind-numbing combinations which she had achieved as a younger woman.

Jennifer could not hold back for long so the moment the formalities were over, the lunch ordered and a decent bottle of claret on the table, she spoke rapidly and quietly to her friend, whose gasps and squeals rather tended to draw more attention to their table than Jennifer wanted.

"What, real spies ? " squeaked Melanie. Never in her life had she been so close to the unreported events of higher politics and she was clutching her glass of wine as if her life depended on it. Only occasionally did she remember to take a sip, so enthralled was she by Jennifer's account of the spooks' visit.

"But that Isaac is a slimy toad. He's capable of anything Jenny, darling. But what if he's the father ? You could never live with that, surely ?"

"I think Michael has enough on him to finish his public career – and probably whichever marriage he's on," said Jennifer. " But would he want to do that to his natural father ?"

Chapter forty-five

Michael's article on Eden James gained much from the colourful language of its subject yet once again was an accurate reflection of their conversation and allowed much of James's artistic licence in his account of his early days.

It largely dwelt on his achievements in advertising and left him basking in professional glory and a little personal roguishness, which barely scratched the surface of his industry reputation for low-end behaviour, at his gaudy villa in the South of France.

No-one was more surprised than James himself when friends telephoned him with the news. He had a copy of the article faxed to his home and grinned with pleasure as he read it.

He was already late for another airport run, so he grabbed the piece of paper, his satellite phone and eased himself into the Ferrari to take a friend of his back to Nice airport with less than enough time to make the London flight.

As the car roared along the autoroute James fiddled with his phone and finally reached Michael in his office. Yelling above the noise of rushing air and traffic being passed he said to Michael: "I mis-judged you lad. That was a nice one. No mention of old tarts or nothing."

Michael was saying "Less of the 'old tart' when you're talking about my mother......." when James screamed "oh fuck............!"

Michael sat in his office, ashen, as he listened to Eden James and his companion die instantly in the tangled wreckage of the Ferrari, whose body-shell disintegrated as it slammed into stationary traffic on the French motorway.

Moments later the call, too, went dead.

At first Jennifer screamed when Michael told her about the accident and added that a Reuters wire had confirmed the death of her former lover. She had shared so much with that man – been a second wife in many respects over a period of years in her youth and, no matter how awful the events he orchestrated against her body, she still nursed a soft spot for him.

"Oh my God ! What have we let ourselves in for here ? First the secret service come banging on my door and now Eden is dead. "

Michael gently suggested to her that there was some sense of rough justice in the untimely way in which Eden had met his fate.

"No, that's a horrible way to go. And what about the poor chap with him. He didn't ask to get smashed to pieces did he ? "

Michael continued to talk quietly to her until she calmed down. He personally was somewhat indifferent to the fate of this rather odious man and he hoped fervently that he would not turn out be his father.

Eventually Jennifer restored her sense of proportion and settled her emotion. "He was a bugger," she said, "but a likeable old sod. Certainly knew how to live – and die, I suppose, wrapped in a Ferrari.

"I wonder if we will be mourning the death of your father ?"

Chapter forty-six

Michael remained furious about the scare his mother had had at the hands of the men in grey, but time, as ever, had a way of putting context around such emotions to enable him to think more clearly and decide on appropriate action.

For those seeking to draw attention to themselves, the "oxygen of publicity," was essential and the best method of denying them their moment in the spotlight was to hose down media attention.

But for those already in the spotlight, to a greater or lesser extent, who sought to use their profile, and whatever power it accrued for them, to force submission from others by stealth, or by blatant corruption of that power as in the case of ranking MPs, an equally stealthy dose of publicity could be a potent antidote.

Michael made a phone call from his office and identified himself to a writer in Soho. As he put the phone down at the end of a lengthy call he smiled because he felt that he had planted the seed that would do for Isaac Kernow

The few paragraphs in 'HP Sauce' in the satirical magazine Private Eye seemed innocuous enough.

'DCMS tea-boy Isaac Kernow MP survived a strong whiff of scandal in his home city of Leicester when he adroitly resigned just before a report linking him to favours for various local businessmen was published back in the eighties.

'But now it seems those days may be coming back to haunt him for another reason. A legend for turning up at the opening of an envelope, despite his reputation with the opposite sex, Isaac, it seems, may have another story to tell.

'The recent hagiography by Michael Leake in the Chronicle polished Isaac's image up, to the MP's obvious delight. But the word in the Members tea-room at the H of C is that there was more to the interview than appeared in print .

'A lady joined the interview between Kernow and Leake, which prompted Isaac to disappear faster than the proverbial rat up a drainpipe, hurling threats of annihilation at the journalist and setting the tea-cups rattling on the Terrace.

'Who could the mystery lady be? We think we should be told. And was there any connection between that interview and the surprise visit of secret agents to the home of West London socialite Jennifer Hawes in Chiswick's fashionable Bedford Park a few days after publication?

'Ms Hawes is known to have an East Midlands background and is a renowned hostess of some of the more unmissable parties on the London scene.

'Is the Government really paranoid enough to let the spooks loose to cover a junior Minister's blushes ?

'Shurely shome mistake !'

Questions in the House for the Secretary of State at the DCMS became very embarrassing for the Minister after the publication of Private Eye and Isaac Kernow adopted a very low profile for a few weeks.

"That at least evens the score," Michael told his mother. "I don't think you'll be troubled by the undercover boys again for a while."

Michael was confident because he knew that he still had a trick or two up his sleeve, which could more than embarrass the junior Minister and MP for Leicester South.

Chapter forty-seven

Jeremy joined Michael at his mother's house later that same evening and the following day they set off together in Jeremy's BMW for Northamptonshire.

Their destination was Winscombe Hall, the seat and stately home of Jamie Avonborough who had invited them to a shoot and an overnight stay so that Michael could interview him for his column.

There were already a dozen cars on the gravel apron before the great doors of the Hall. Jamie was sitting on the stone balustrade to one side of the stairs to the entrance talking to two other men, similarly dressed in tweeds, elbow patches, plus-fours and Wellington boots.

Jeremy eased the BMW between a sports Bentley and an Aston Martin Vantage and affected a nonchalant air as he and Michael crunched across the gravel towards their host.

"Excuse me, chaps," said Jamie to his companions, "but I've two members of the Fourth Estate to greet here. I'll be back." With that he moved swiftly down the steps to greet: "Michael ? How are you ? Welcome to Winscombe Hall.

"Let Johnston take your bags to your rooms and get yourselves ready for the shoot. We're stepping off in a few minutes. Ever done this sort of thing before ? "

Michael had not, but Jeremy had been clay-pigeon shooting a few times so had some reasonable knowledge of handling a gun.

"I expect some of these fellows will be a bit wild," said Jamie quietly. "They're mostly from America and some distant parts of Europe. But they pay well and the estate always needs the money ! I'm just here to meet and greet and have m'picture taken !

"Just enjoy the day. There'll be hampers at lunch-time and plenty of grog to keep you going. We can have a chat this evening after dinner and finish off tomorrow if necessary. I wanted you to see the estate in action and get a feel for country life before we get the words down."

His man then handed Michael and Jeremy a shotgun apiece and a handful of shells. He showed them how to carry the guns, broken, over their shoulders or across their arm until they were in position and he cautioned them about when and how to shoot

Jamie Avonborough was good value for his customers, striding from one group to another, his gamekeeper within reach, and encouraging them to bag as many birds as they could.

Michael actually shot a partridge but Jeremy was none too keen on the whole affair and deliberately aimed low. Even so he was credited with a pheasant by lunch-time.

The best part of the day was the big hot tub before dinner. Tramping about the countryside can cover quite a few miles and the copious number of 'snorts' from various hip-flasks and bottles led to quite a boozy haze by four o'clock. Michael felt fine because he tended to opt for water and left the fiery stuff to Jeremy who was distinctly the worse for wear by the time the groups re-convened at the house around 4.30p.m. – he was not alone.

But everyone was swiftly packed off to their respective bathrooms and given robes in which to relax for an hour or two before aperitifs at 6.30p.m.

Dinner became a boisterous affair with the Americans and the Germans vying for loudest and most offensive groups. Avonborough smiled benignly as many of them stumbled off to bed quite early being incapable of further speech or song.

"Care to join me in the library ?" he said to Michael. "We can talk in peace there."

Jeremy had learnt the lesson of the day and interspersed his evening wine with glasses of water, thus remaining quite compos mentis for the latter part of the evening.

"Not a bad lifestyle for a country bigwig," began Michael. "But I suppose there is much more to it than meets the eye, as ever."

"Indeed," said Jamie. " There's actually a huge amount of bloody work involved in managing an estate these days. You've got to be a farmer, an accountant, a land manager, a conservationist, an expert on European law and a father figure for all the people whose jobs depend on you getting it right.

"Sure there's value in the land, but value doesn't pay bills and wages, so we've all got to find ways of keeping these places going when we're taxed out of sight and hog tied with EU legislation."

"But surely there's some pleasure in living in a huge house like this that has been in your family for generations and looking out the window at your own land for as far as you can see ? Have you any idea what it's like to live on a council estate ?"

"Pretty bloody grim, I suppose," conceded Jamie, soberly.

The conversation ranged over every facet of country life and some of the ideas which Jamie Avonborough was attempting to develop on his estate – not least organic farming and related products which he proudly proclaimed were doing "very well indeed."

Jamie took Michael and Jeremy on a tour of the day rooms of the house. His study was in one corner with double aspect windows looking south and west. The views across his land were impressive and might have stimulated a more creative intellect.

But he led the two brothers straight across the room to the door to his inner sanctum - his second, more private, study.

"Now, this bit is strictly off the record and you must promise me that you will not mention it or I will not take you in there. Even my wife has never been in this room."

He smiled conspiratorially and unlocked the door. The room was smaller and much darker than the study with only one quite small window with a curtain pulled across it.

When Jamie Avonborough switched on the light both Michael and Jeremy gasped as the painted ceiling revealed an eighteenth century orgy in full swing, setting the theme for the whole room. Everything, from small tapestries on the wall, to paintings, sculptures and books was devoted to sex, and largely deviant sex at that.

Featured before the darkened window was a large, flat-screen television "for the DVDs" motioned Jamie. "Do you want to see one ?" he pressed a button and immediately a latter-day scene of orgiastic contortions flashed on to the screen,

Jamie giggled almost shame-facedly at the revelation of his secret room and even Jeremy felt slightly overwhelmed as it appeared to him that no aspect of sexual behaviour between adults – and thank goodness that was where the line had been drawn – had been overlooked in this room.

"So, where's the dungeon?" smiled Jeremy, as the trio vacated the room to return to the library.

"There used to be one," said Jamie as he carefully locked the inner study door. " Apparently my grandfather was quite keen on a bit of flagellation and bondage, but it was taken out many years ago and we've had to make do with this little lot ever since."

"This might be a good time, then," said Michael," to bring up your own taste in parties. Would you call yourself a swinger, Jamie ?"

"Well........." paused Jamie for almost a minute, " Petronella and I love a good party and when we were a bit younger before the kids came along I suppose we used to get around the county a bit to one party or another."

"I hear you were a regular at Ray and Sarah Barnes' little gatherings in Belsingham, near the castle, in the eighties."

Avonborough shot him a quick glance from beneath a furrowed brow. Why was he bringing up those parties?

"You were pretty much part of the crowd there, weren't you?" persisted Michael. "You and the Prince, Eden James, Isaac Kernow and Clancy Turner – weren't you the boys, so to speak?

"By the way, did you hear that Eden James had died? Smashed his Ferrari into a line of stationary traffic on the French motorway a couple of weeks ago."

"Oh my God!" said Avonborough, visibly shaken. "He was so much fun, Eden. I saw your article on him – very true to life. Hadn't seen him for a good long time. I think he spent most of his time in the South of France didn't he?"

"Apparently so," said Michael. You boys had a bit of a party down there too from time to time, I gather?"

"Well, there was a time when we all – wives and children included – spent much of August at Eden's place. He had a great pool and was not too far from the coast. But since the children have got older, they tend to holiday in their own way and we have been too busy with the estate to be away so much.

"Anyway," Jamie was refreshed having steered the conversation a bit away from his party habits, " that was all a long time ago and has very little to do with managing today's rural habitat, which is what you said you wanted to talk about."

"Yes, of course," replied Michael. "That is all good stuff for the feature and what I am talking about now is more personal in nature and not likely to find exposure in the paper – at least not yet anyway.

"Tell me, was Pamela Gerber among your acquaintances at the Barnes' parties?"

"Gosh, now you're asking," said Jamie somewhat disingenuously, " one met so many people on those occasions. Let me think, the name does ring a tiny bell. I hope you're not implying that I might have had an affair with this woman, or something. Because, despite what you may have seen in my private study, I have never actually been unfaithful to my wife and I am rather proud of that."

"I guess it depends how you define 'unfaithful'," Michael mused aloud. "does participating in gang-rape, as opposed to trying to prevent it, count as unfaithful in your book?"

Jamie Avonborough jumped to his feet with a look of fury on his face. "That's it – interview over. Goodnight." And he strode out of the library, slamming the door behind him. Michael and Jeremy looked at one another in stunned disbelief. It seems Michael had hit a nerve by suggesting that Avonborough might have prevented the attack on his mother, and didn't.

"Ah well, another seed planted," said Jeremy dispassionately as he picked up Avonborough's glass, wrapped it lightly in his handkerchief and pocketed it.

The following morning neither Michael nor Jeremy saw Jamie Avonborough, but his wife Petronella's demeanour didn't suggest anything unusual. "Haven't seen him myself, " she said brightly over kippers and scrambled eggs in the dining room. "But he often goes out early in the morning with the dogs."

So Michael and Jeremy, complete with booty from Winscombe Hall, settled back into Jeremy's car for the return journey to London.

They had almost arrived when Michael's office contacted his mobile telephone. He and his brother were shocked to learn that Jamie Avonborough had been discovered shot dead in the woods near his home. His dogs were standing guard over him.

Worse, the Northamptonshire police were apparently rather anxious to speak to Michael and his brother, as it would appear that they were the last people to see the man alive.

The editor of the Chronicle came on the line: "Michael, I know it's tough if the chap was a friend of yours, but you'd better get back there and find out what you can. Clearly we will have to spike the feature, unless you can spin it as the last thoughts of an aristo in the shit or something like that.

"Get us a couple of hundred words as soon as poss after you get there if there's anything interesting, but don't queer the pitch for the cops. Sounds like suicide, but why ? Bye."

Jeremy pulled into the London Gateway Services close to the London end of the M1. The two young men needed a strong coffee and a moment or two to gather their thoughts.

Even as he walked towards the busy services entrance, Michael's phone rang again. The Northamptonshire police did, indeed, want to interview him and Jeremy as soon as possible. Michael assured them that they were turning round to return to Winscombe Hall and would be there in a couple of hours.

He telephoned his mother, who shrieked at the news of another death. "Oh no, I can't stand this any more. What happened to him ? We can't go on like this. Everyone I've ever known seems to be dying or getting killed in some terrible way. Michael that has to be the finish of this !"

"I know it's apparently a real tragedy, but now we've started this hunt for my father we can't just switch it off. I'm really sorry that a couple of your former friends have died in less than ideal circumstances, but I still want to know who my father is – or was, replied Michael in firm but measured tones. He didn't want to upset his mother any further, especially as he was still getting to know her after 25 years, but the investigation had to go on to a conclusion. He was adamant about that.

"Poor dear man !" continued Jennifer. "Of any of them he was the least aggressive and behaved more like a puppy with me. We never.........you know !"

"Well, that confirms one part of his story," said Michael grimly. "But don't forget he participated in that disgraceful attack on you, or at least did nothing to try and prevent it.

"I must say it's no fun being the prime suspect in a suspicious death. But we're going back to Northamptonshire to find out what happened. It seems on the surface to have been suicide, but who knows ?"

Jeremy and Michael drove in complete silence back up the 50 miles or so to Jamie Avonborough's estate. Neither could quite reconcile the savage termination of a life which, while it may have contributed little other than a continuity of employment for estate workers, certainly didn't cause any major harm to society.

Jeremy negotiated the policeman guarding the street entrance to the estate and drove up the drive to the gravel apron before Winscombe Hall. In addition to the Bentleys and the Aston Martins there were sundry police cars, marked and unmarked; policemen in and out of uniform but all wearing luminous yellow vests emblazoned with 'POLICE' across the back with a smaller flash on the front and a Command Post vehicle.

" Seems as though the death of the Lord of the Manor is big bananas up here," offered Jeremy rather insensitively.

The pair were immediately escorted to the senior officer who, in a scene straight from Agatha Christie, was in the drawing room with seven or eight people sitting around, including Avonborough's widow Petronella, red-eyed but already changed into a demure black outfit.

The police had gathered plenty of incidental anecdotal evidence up to the point where participants at the previous evening's dinner, including his wife, had gone to bed or watched as Avonborough shepherded Jeremy and Michael out of the dining room to, apparently, the library.

There the trail ran cold, so to speak, until the return of the two brothers.

Michael insisted on a private interview with the superintendent of the local police, so he and Jeremy adjourned with him and a young constable to take notes, to the library – again.

Michael gave a full account of their conversation the previous evening and acknowledged that he had been probing rumours of possible misbehaviour some 20 to 30 years earlier when Avonborough had stormed out of the interview.

That was the last he had seen of the landowner, as Jeremy confirmed, and he had not been apparent earlier that morning, so they left. The police officer seemed content with Michael's explanation and declared the interview at an end, thanking them for returning so promptly.

They were about to make their exit when Jeremy enquired casually: "Do you think it was suicide, or did one of these mad Yanks kill him with friendly fire?"

The policeman grimaced at the doubtful taste of Jeremy's remark, but added: " I shouldn't really tell you this, but there was a note with the body – something about not being able to bear the responsibility – so we're pretty sure it was self-inflicted. The position of the shotgun was also indicative of suicide. I assume he was worried about the estate or something.

"But that's for the coroner to decide. You will be notified in due course about where to go for that. Thank you again, gentlemen."

"Well………," said Jeremy and Michael almost in unison when they returned to Jeremy's car. They did not speak again until they had passed the policeman at the gate, who offered a slight salute as they went by, and they were well on the way back to the motorway.

Chapter forty-eight

One death from a group of erstwhile friends may seem unfortunate, normal even, but two within a few weeks is sufficient to catch some sharp eyes and, having been alerted several weeks before to the circumstances of Isaac Kernow's interview with Michael Leake, the ever-watchful scribes of Private Eye were quick to surmise on the connections between interviews by Michael Leake, death, and the socialite Jennifer Hawes who appeared to know all the participants.

The inquest into the Duke of Avonborough's death barely merited a paragraph in the national dailies. Suicide it was, then, despite the ambiguity of the note found with the body. The police view prevailed and what had been potentially a society scandal faded from the pages of the newspapers rather more quickly than it had arrived.

But little strands and rumours were persisting and being picked up and pieced together by the small but assiduous staff at Private Eye, and within a couple of issues after the Avonborough inquest verdict, the columns of this influential journal returned to haunt Isaac Kernow.

'More tidbits of information linking junior Minister at the DCMS Isaac Kernow and a party-going set in his native East Midlands have emerged in recent days.

'Renowned for his addiction to parties and pretty women, Isaac, who is on his third 'partner,' his ex-wife's former best friend, may seem to have something that he would not care to be made public in his distant past.

'Kernow, MP for Leicester South, was well-known on the party circuit in the East Midlands in the eighties and resigned as leader of his local council just before rumours of 'bungs' and favours surfaced among his circle of friends, which included many of the best-known businessmen and women of the two counties – Leicestershire and Northamptonshire.

'Now two of his set have died in recent weeks – both after interviews with leading journalist Michael Leake, with whom Kernow had the minor fracas at the House of Commons a couple of months ago.

'We hear that West London socialite Jennifer Hawes, who is dating Michael's elder brother Jeremy, a sometime pop impresario, also knew the trio – Kernow, Eden James, an adman who crashed his Ferrari spectacularly on the French Riviera with fatal consequences, and Jamie Avonborough who recently committed suicide at his ancestral home, Winscombe Hall.

' Shurely shome connection ? Perhaps Mr Kernow knows more than he cares to admit.'

The like-minded and committed community of Private Eye readers seized on this short single-column piece – among them a number of Fleet Street hacks who kept their employment largely by following-up similar such intriguing suggestions in the magazine.

Utilising their vastly greater resources, several of the national dailies at the lower end of the journalism spectrum were able to uncover suggestions of sexual impropriety involving all three, possibly more, and Ms Jennifer Hawes.

For the moment each held back on using Jennifer's name in their pieces, referring only to a local public relations woman from the East Midlands who had travelled to the South of France and had possibly been badly treated by the fun-loving trio. But one less cautious 'red-top' did allude to a well-known socialite being involved.

But they did not spare the limelight from the junior minister at the DCMS, who came under siege to absolve himself from the innuendo and rumour beginning to creep across the columns of the scandal-driven press. Radio and television, as was their wont, hardly mentioned the highly speculative story – until opposition MPs began to ask questions in the House. Had the House been misled by earlier responses by the Minister regarding his altercation with a journalist within the precincts of the House? Would the Minister care to comment on allegations of involvement in a sex party in the South of France before his election?

Parliamentary privilege exonerates MPs from laws of libel or slander within the precincts of the Westminster estate and the tabloid press gleefully reported every word for their celebrity scandal readerships.

Jennifer came under immense pressure at her London home with media camped outside, photographing her every move. But, for the moment she was saying nothing beyond a slight smile and an acknowledging movement of the hand, whenever she left or returned to her home behind the ever-present dark glasses.

Some papers fuelled the saga with recollections of the Profumo scandal some 40 years earlier with allegations of various activities involving call-girls, prostitutes, and Russian spies. Spies were a little thin on the ground with this one, as were prostitutes, but an attractive socialite with a history, dating a much younger man whose brother was a leading journalist, all linked to a couple of deaths, one admittedly accidental, and a junior Government Minister – where could it lead?

If Jennifer experienced some inconvenience and a little pressure, it was nothing compared to Isaac's ordeal by a circling pack of predatory journalists. More than a dozen had taken up permanent station outside his Wandsworth home with a few more keeping an eye on his constituency home in Leicester.

They and half-a-dozen television crews from stations in various parts of the globe were grateful for the proximity of the Wandsworth house to a pub, serving decent food throughout the day. A solid rota system was soon adopted allowing the Fourth Estate to remain refreshed at all times.

It took three days, including support from his Secretary of State and endorsements from the Prime Minister and other Party worthies, for Isaac to cave in and resign.

His resignation speech from the back-benches in the Commons was a model of craven self-absolution and denial with frequent familiar toadying phrases of support for his erstwhile Cabinet friends. And then he was gone – from the media and any prospect of a glittering political career, which he had so assiduously carved out. He was finished.

Chapter forty-nine

Mysteriously Jennifer's computer was delivered back to her by a cheery young man in an unmarked van, a few days after Isaac's resignation. "Apparently they don't need this any more in the office," he remarked cryptically as he handed over the lap-top to Jennifer and sped off.

Sam Leake along with Jeremy and Michael had witnessed the visit and return of the machine as all four discussed the situation in the light of Michael's quest to identify his natural father.

"I never thought it would become this public or this messy," said Sam, who had managed to keep well in the background the whole time, although he was concerned for Michael's profile and reputation. Strangely Jeremy's seemed to be enhanced within the entertainment industry and he was quite a celebrity among his peers in that community.

"We have DNA results back on Kernow and Eden James and they're locked away. Even I haven't seen the results yet ! We know that we will get a sample from Jamie Avonborough.

"But, my goodness, at what price are these samples coming ? One career ruined already, and two deaths, one self-inflicted by all accounts. And these may not be the guilty man – apart from perhaps their attitude to life and that really regrettable incident in which they were all involved.

"Now we move into the Premier League with Clancy Turner, because he is a major player in the biggest game in the world – American politics. The publicity here will not help your cause and it may be difficult now to draw him in to an interview situation. Please move very slowly and carefully. The British secret services are pussy-cats compared to their American counterparts who tend to shoot before they speak."

Chapter fifty

"Melanie, I can't help feeling guilty about these guys, you know ? " said Jennifer over coffee. " In one way I feel a little bit vindicated because they were such pigs to me, but it does seem terrible to lose your life over it. After all, I didn't die, and I have been re-united with my baby. "

Melanie's colour rose as, for once, she became deadly serious. " Jenny, these guys have played fast and loose all their lives. They've treated other people like cattle to be shoved around at will and then knocked off when dinner time calls.

"Get real, girl. They treated you like a piece of shit, just because they were pissed and full of testosterone. There's no excuse for that. You're about as guilty as Adam and Eve – before they bit the bloody apple.

"You can't expect to live life the way they have done – and us to some extent – without it hitting back in some shape or form. I may have been a bit reckless but Ted knows I love him and the kids more than anything and he is generous enough to let me get the madness out of my system without recrimination. Perhaps that's why I still love him so much. But I've never set out to hurt him and I don't think you have ever set out to hurt anyone.

"There's rules to life. Nobody really knows what they are but I guess it's something like treating people with respect, or doing unto others what you would have done to yourself, in a way.

"You've never double-crossed a husband. You may have mixed up a few lovers here and there but you hadn't made any particular commitment to them or they to you. And with Martin you had an acknowledged – and two-way – understanding, rather like Ted and I, that what the eye doesn't see, the heart – whatever.

"Except Ted likes me to tell him," she giggled. "So don't be a stupid tart and start blaming yourself for the misbehaviour of others who tried to bend the rules, such as they are, too far."

Jennifer stared almost open-mouthed at her confidante who had never quite read the riot act to her in such a way before. But she touched Melanie lightly on the arm and said: "Thank you. That makes me feel more relaxed about it. You're right, of course.

"But we've still one more of the gang of four to confront and this could be the trickiest of the lot. Clancy was gorgeous. He was fun, a terrific lover – I could feel his touch for days afterwards – and a really, really nice man. But I will never forget that look of out-of-control blazing lust in his eyes in France. That was terrifying.

"I think I will go with Michael and Jeremy to the States for this because it could be very difficult for them. Jerry's unknown there except in some quarters of the music business and that's no protection and Michael has only the slight power of the media, but what do they know of the British newspapers over there – or care. "

Chapter fifty-one

Jennifer treated Jeremy to a seat in business class on their return flight to Los Angeles, so that they could be near the expenses-based Michael, whose elevation to this superior travel allowance reflected the senior management's approval of the impact of his column.

Contacting Clancy Turner for an interview had been surprisingly easy. It appeared that the circumstances around the resignation of a British junior Minister – and the act of resignation itself – were of no consequence to the firmly fawning American media with its sights firmly focused on Washington and blissfully unaware of anything happening in the former Mother country.

So Clancy rather jumped at the opportunity to gain profile in the British media after his good times 20 years or more earlier. He had managed his departure from the country at least as well as he managed everything else in his professional life as an attorney in business.

Nobody in the United States could have been aware of the slightest blemish on his moral integrity, the strength of which had propelled him to high office in the Administration these past three years.

He and his wife were regulars on the Washington dinner party circuit and much admired as icons of African-American advancement in the inner circles of American politics.

But he took care to fit the interview in during a visit to California where he knew that he could spare sufficient time to make the thing work to his own satisfaction , and that he would be well away from the insatiably prying eyes of Washington – and his wife.

He had been briefed, at least, on the background of Michael Leake and he understood that his brother Jeremy often sat in on interviews and acted as a kind of gofer for him – a job he apparently pursued professionally in the music business. But, no matter, if he was to build himself a profile and a cuttings library to support a Presidential bid in a few years time, he needed this interview to go well. And the Chronicle was a decent enough paper in the middle ground of British media.

His small but ostentatious motorcade pulled into the driveway of the Beverly Hills Hotel, where his travelling secret servicemen were joined by the two advance party men who had checked the place out in the 24 hours prior to his arrival. Standard form, he mused, as he waited for his passenger door to be opened by another armed guard.

The Attorney-General of the United States of America was greeted by the hotel manager profusely. He grinned, shook hands and moved forward quickly to enter the hotel through a lobby that had been cleared by his aides and on into the gardens where his sponsored, detached bungalow was situated.

"Hey, we got Elizabeth Taylor's place, " he grinned to his private secretary. "Love those gold taps." He pitched himself onto a large floral-print sofa in the living room of this exquisite but complete building alongside many others in the grounds of the hotel, and began to work through papers whilst awaiting his visitors from the U.K.

Chapter fifty-two

"Coffee, sir?" was the question but the voice was startlingly familiar to Jeremy. Barbara Andrews ! He looked up, she did a double-take, and the coffee spilt neatly into his lap, causing a momentary splash of pain.

"This is where I came in, I think, " said Jeremy screwing himself up in his seat in a bid to lessen the pain of the hot coffee. Jennifer took in the scene at a glance, as Barbara produced a small cloth amid profuse apologies delivered in the tightest professional voice.

"Friend of yours?" she said with an air of amusement both at the accident and the encounter.

"Not really, she was in steerage on my last trip out here to meet you – and believe it or not some Scotch was spilled into my lap then."

"Remarkable dear. How did she get promoted to business class with a record like that. Did you recommend her?" Jennifer was still enjoying the whole affair, now that she was sure that Jeremy was not unduly hurt.

He clambered to his feet and headed for the galley in business class, where Barbara was standing with her hands clasped either side of her nose as she finished recounting their history to the slender and smiling steward.

"I really am sorry, Jerry, " she said warmly. "I can't believe it's happened again – and this time with hot coffee ! Are you OK ? Who's that you're travelling with, anyway, your mother ?"

Jeremy winced. "No, I'm with my brother and she's a friend of ours."

"Looks to be a bit more than a friend if you ask me," retorted Barbara. "Still, who cares? You'll be at the Beverly Hills, I suppose, if a sudden insane impulse sweeps over me. Unlikely, I assure you. I've sent Christian to First Class to fetch a robe for you. He will then sponge and dry your trousers for you sir, and I can't tell you how sorry I am once again." Her voice swung from friendship to professional within the space of a couple of sentences. And with that she returned to her duties and never spoke to Jeremy again for the duration of the flight.

Christian came back with a robe and whisked away Jerry's trousers with a flourish when he had effected the change.

Jeremy sat down to face his grinning brother across the aisle and a still amused Jennifer. He alone was not amused. "Blondes with a neat little tush, eh ?" sparkled Jennifer. Jeremy subsided into a black mood and stared obsessively at his miniature cinema screen.

After a couple of hours, Christian the slim steward appeared before Jeremy with his pressed, clean, dried trousers on a hangar. "Voila, monsieur," he announced triumphantly. "I hope you will find my efforts satisfactory ?"

Jeremy managed a slightly amused 'thank you' at this dramatic affectation and smiled. Christian was actually quite attractive. A sharp finger into his buttock as he stood up reminded him who he was travelling with – and why.

As the trio were exiting the aircraft, Barbara leant forward to Jeremy: " Box of matches, sir, compliments of the airline?" He grimaced at the joke and mumbled "touch " as he set off up the gantry towards the arrivals lounge, popping the matches into his top jacket pocket, as before.

At the Beverly Hills Hotel, Jeremy waited until Jennifer was in the shower before he took the matches from his pocket and opened the flap. 'You are a snake – but call me if you like ! Bx' He carefully replaced the matches.

Chapter fifty-three

Dinner a trois for Jennifer and the Leake boys was a fresh seafood feast of oysters and scallops from the Pacific served with the freshest of iceberg lettuce salad in Jeremy and Jennifer's suite.

They chatted over the following day's meeting and debated whether or not Jennifer should put in an appearance. They decided against it and she agreed to lie low in the room while the conversation took place out in the bungalow in the grounds.

Finally, tired from the flight, Jennifer and Jeremy opted for bed and Michael retired to his room next door.

Promptly at 10a.m. the next morning, Jeremy and Michael became aware of two young men with earpieces and dark glasses materialising alongside them in the hotel breakfast area beyond the Polo Lounge. Jennifer had remained in the room and breakfasted alone on pink grapefruit and toast with a little orange 'confiture.' Sadly, no marmalade.

"Gentlemen, " said suit number one quietly, "if you are ready, the Attorney General of the United States is waiting. Please follow us."

Follow was certainly true of the one, but the other fell in behind Jeremy and Michael and murmured into his wrist. "Visitor party en route. ETA two minutes."

The Leake brothers smiled at the absurdly officious and paranoid way in which the Attorney-General's security was ordered. Nevertheless they kept step through the lobby and out into the garden. Once outside the immediate building, suit number one said: "Please stop here, gentlemen."

And before they went a step further he and his colleague thoroughly frisked Jeremy and Michael, searching into any pocket with the slightest bulging content.

"Thank you gentlemen, please proceed." And on they went past two more suits loitering near the door of a bungalow at which suit number two knocked.

"Come on in," the smiling face of Clancy Turner emerged before his words were complete. "Thanks, boys." He nodded to the suits who took up station outside the front door of the bungalow.

"Now then, which one of you is Michael?"

As great as his stature was in the United States, Clancy remained flattered to be approached by a serious British newspaper, the Chronicle, in what he understood to be an ongoing series on personalities of the future by Michael Leake. He was anxious to please this seemingly diffident young writer from Great Britain.

The conversation ranged across Clancy's brilliant career as a lawyer, first in corporate circles and then moving into political connections before inevitably taking a step across the narrow divide between the two into politics full-time.

Michael enjoyed his frankness in comparison to many of the English interviews which he had conducted and, like so many before him, was charmed by this fit, handsome man who was clearly in control of his life and his destiny.

But cracks began to appear in that perma-smooth exterior when Michael started to probe his days in England. Why had a high-powered American corporate lawyer devoted so much time to a failing steel industry around Cranby in the East Midlands of England?

Why had he pursued such a wide range of contacts and worked the social scene so zealously ?

"Well, the answer to your first question is simple. Bechtel Corporation was interested – is interested – in any large-scale development, or re-development. The company has well-developed expertise in regeneration of regions.

"The closing of the steelworks in and around Cranby created a vast area of land in a strategically strong positioning in the United Kingdom. Of course Bechtel was interested in talking to the local community, the elected representatives in the region and the national Government to see how it could help in the re-generation of the greater area.

"I guess the answer to your second question there is a little tougher," he smiled that dazzling white smile set against his light-brown skin. "We Americans, or at least some of 'we Americans' " the smile flashing again," like to work real hard and play just as hard – to get the most out of life, I guess.

"I was a bit of a jock in High School, you know, captain of the football team and all that. At University I took it to another level. I have always had a kinda zest for life, so it's natural for me to focus first on the work – and then on the play. I don't see that as something to be apologetic about."

"Maybe not," said Michael, "but when there's a strong suspicion that those you are playing with have an agenda, and that agenda may work against public interest then surely the play takes on another, more sinister dimension."

"What the hell are you drivin' at?" said Clancy, still smiling a slightly more set smile, but pleasant enough.

"You were particularly close to people like Isaac Kernow, the leader of Leicester City Council at the time. And it seems a remarkable coincidence that you left town, and the country, just before allegations of corruption were levelled against him and he resigned. Did you know that ?"

"Hey, you can't stick that one on me ! " exclaimed Clancy, still thoroughly in control of his emotions and smiling throughout, although the smile was beginning to freeze in reptilian fashion.

"Of course I knew Isaac. It was part of my job to know him – a big part. I heard when I got back to the States from our people in England that he had resigned but I understood he was going to take a run for Parliament. Did he not do that ?"

"Oh yes, and he has just resigned again – as a junior Minister in the Government. Did you know that ?"

"No way !" lied Clancy. " Why did he do that ?"

"Well, he was linked again to some undesirable behaviour in that same period in the eighties and the clamour in the press in England grew to such a level that he was forced to withdraw from the Government."

"Wow, it must have been something heavy. What was all that about ?"

Jeremy pitched in to the conversation: "His mother" gesturing towards Michael.

"I thought you two guys were brothers ?"

"We are, in a sense" said Jeremy," but Michael is my step-brother. He was adopted by my family at birth."

"Oh, I see. So Isaac had a scene with your mother and it only got discovered recently and he was forced to resign for being a naughty boy, eh ? You English are so inhibited about sex."

"And you Americans are not, I suppose," cut in Michael. "You only have to look at the Bible belt, the Creationists and the prudery of your television here."

"Hell, that's a whole different discussion. Guys, it's been great, but I gotta move on swiftly here," said Clancy deftly wrapping up the proceedings.

"Just one last question," insisted Michael. "How well did you know Pamela Gerber in those early days, and did you ever meet her in the South of France?"

"Goddammit " Clancy exploded in fury and smashed his fist down on what he thought was going to be the table. Instead he caught the edge of his tumbler of water, smashing the glass and cutting his hand.

Jeremy jumped forward, grabbing a few tissues from a box on the table and swathed Turner's hand in them. "Thanks, " he muttered, immediately taking control of his temper again.

The commotion caused suits one and two to burst in through the front door. "OK boss ?" It could have been a Hollywood movie – in Beverly Hills.

Clancy waved them away and removed the tissues from his hand, which had only been slightly cut. He kicked a few pieces of bloodstained glass away from the table and ignored the mess.

"Pamela Gerber ? Sure I knew her. Everyone on the social scene around Belsingham and Leicester knew Pam. She was a great gal, and a smart business woman. But I'm a married man, Mr Leake, and the other Mr Leake, if you have the same name. I did not have any relations with Miss Gerber. My wife knew her too, from the various parties and her company used to handle some PR issues for me. That's all.

"Why do you pick her out of the crowd ? Was <u>she</u> the downfall of Isaac Kernow - I can't believe that !" the smile returned to brighten but disguise his features.

"Pamela Gerber is my mother, Mr Turner," said Michael through thin lips.

"Woah, that's it, time to call a halt to this," called Clancy. " It's been great, guys, but let's not get deep down into personal issues like that. I'm sorry if your mother is involved with some messy politics in England but leave me out, OK? " He leaned forward close to Michael's face. "And I mean, leave me out, do you understand me?"

"Oh, I think so," said Michael in his calm and measured way. " We'll be on our way now. Don't worry about the feature. It will reflect well on you. People in England are always interested in the movers and shakers of American politics."

Clancy stood up, affability restored "Sure, guys. Thanks again." Almost unnoticed the two suits had stepped back inside the door. Either there was a secret signal somewhere about Clancy's person or they had been listening in all along.

No-one spoke as the foursome threaded its way back along the stone paths and evergreen foliage among the Beverly Hills Hotel bungalows, but Michael managed a one eyebrow quizzical look at Jeremy who smiled silently and nodded.

In the lobby the security detail excused themselves: "Thank you, gentlemen" and vanished back into the gardens.

Jeremy and Michael pressed impatiently for the elevator to take them two floors up to the room where Jennifer awaited their return.

"Wow, he's a big smoothie ! " said Jeremy. "But I didn't fancy that smile – looked like an alligator !"

Jennifer smiled reflectively as Michael gave an account of the interview. "It's all pretty good stuff. You know, High School football captain, University hero, corporate wunderkind and clearly now, a political heavyweight. I can't see much stopping him making President in a few years if he wants it badly enough."

"What did he have to say about me ?" she enquired at last.

"Very little to actually say. But he handled it very well. Put on a big show of anger that he, a married man, should somehow be implicated with 'a great gal and a smart businesswoman. My wife knew her, too'

"He smashed a glass with his fist to completely swamp his embarrassment and swiftly brought matters to a conclusion."

"So no admission about the South of France ?"

"He made sure we didn't get there. I did mention it, but that's when the glass-smashing began. Speaks for itself really," concluded Michael.

At this point Jeremy grinned and, once again, produced 'the evidence.' "Tarrah !" he cried, placing two bloodied tissues and a sliver of glass covered in Clancy's blood.

Suddenly Jennifer put her finger to her lips, carefully picked up the tissues and the piece of glass and walked through to the bedroom to put them into her jewelry box. This she then placed in a large shopping carrier bag from Rodeo Drive – she had not entirely wasted her time while the boys did the interview – and walked silently from the room, gesturing the boys to remain silent, too.

She returned a few minutes later with an empty shopping bag and a smile. Once again she put her finger to her lips before saying brightly:" Well, that's that, then. You've done your work, I've done some shopping – let's get dinner organised. I'll get the captain to book us a table.

"You two need to freshen up. Shall we say a couple of hours ? Jolly good."

Jennifer's little charade had alerted Jeremy and Michael – as if they could forget - that the presence of the Attorney General of the United States in the hotel involved a disproportionate number of secret servicemen standing around and slipping in and out of shadows.

The possibility of their room being bugged was quite strong in the circumstances.

It wasn't until they had changed tables several times at their chosen restaurant that Jennifer appeared satisfied with her position and they felt free enough to resume conversation.

"So you have put the evidence, so to speak, where exactly ?' said Jeremy.

"Well, " said Jennifer with a little flourish, copied from Joan Collins," I expect they think I have put my jewelry box into the hotel safe deposit. And so I have, as every sensible girl should."

"But what about the evidence ?" said Jeremy.

Jennifer beamed with closed lips and gently patted the underside of her left breast very discreetly. Both Michael and Jeremy roared with laughter and dinner proceeded at a cracking pace with a slightly end-of-term feel to it since they had now confronted, to one degree or another, all four 'suspects.'

At the end of the meal Jeremy excused himself and said that he wanted to walk the streets for a little while before returning to the hotel. He would grab a taxi later, he said, as a concerned Jennifer and a very relaxed Michael stepped into their chauffeured car.

Jennifer's concern was genuinely for Jeremy's safety. Of course she was aware that he might be using the fresh air, or rather the polluted Los Angeles air, as an excuse to pick up a hooker or a rent boy. But that didn't amount to a row of beans in her book. Everyone was entitled to a little time out. She was used to it over the years. But she had forgotten, momentarily, about Barbara Andrews.

Jeremy headed for the Marriott Hotel, pausing at a pay-phone kiosk on Sunset Boulevard.............

Chapter fifty-four

Michael went happily next door to his room, leaving Jennifer to unlock her door. She stepped inside and recoiled in horror. Someone had been in and turned the place over, there was chaos everywhere. Clearly the room had been very thoroughly searched.

And, surprisingly, there on her bed was her jewelry box, complete with spilled contents. How had that been returned to the room, she wondered ?

Jennifer's brain moved quickly. It was time to get out. She did not bother to alert the hotel management to the break-in, there must have been some complicity by the staff. She simply called down to the desk to ask for her car to return.

She knocked on the door leading directly to Michael's room. In response to his hissed "yes?" she whispered "come in here." They jointly unlocked the common door and Michael stepped into the room. Jennifer immediately put a finger to his lips.

She scribbled on a pad on the living room table. 'Get J back here. Leaving. Midnight flight.'

There was no doubting Jennifer's seriousness and she left the room with her mobile phone to call the airport

There was no reply from Jeremy's phone and Michael left a guarded message which in itself left no doubt about its urgency for Jerry to get back to the hotel.

Both Jennifer and Michael hurriedly packed their bags and Michael quickly processed all of Jeremy's things into his.

Michael whispered urgently to Jennifer: "What about Jerry ?"

"He'll know what we've done. We'll call him again on the way to the airport. You take the bags down to the side road. I'll get the car and come round and pick you up."

At that moment the room telephone rang. Jennifer snatched it up thinking it was Jerry calling. "Hi, Pammy," drawled a familiar rich, oak voice. " I kinda figured if your boy was here you wouldn't be far away. Gotcha in one, babe. How the devil are you ? I'm downstairs in a bungalow. Why don't you come on over and catch up on all those years."

"Clancy, how on earth did you know I was here ?" said Jennifer as sweetly as she could muster.

"It helps to be the Attorney General of the United States," he volunteered somewhat unnecessarily. "Hey, come on over, we need to talk. " he added cheerfully.

"OK," said Jennifer. "Where are you ?"

"A couple of my boys are on the way up to your room now to show you the way, darlin'. Bye"

Jennifer threw the phone down and rushed Michael out of the room. They sped down the stairs, Michael turning to hustle his way out to the side exit as Jennifer affected her nonchalant stroll through the reception area and the genuflecting staff. A few steps down the red carpet and she stepped safely into the back of her car.

"Go, go, go" she hissed at the driver.

"Where to, ma'am ?" came the bemused reply.

"Just get round the corner into North Beverly Drive and pick up my son. Then I'll direct you."

The driver sensed the urgency and was happy to enter into the spirit of this thing, which seemed to him to be some sort of romantic caper.

The car slid urgently round the block and pulled up alongside Michael and several bags, which he had manhandled to this point. He threw them into the front of the car and leapt into the back.

"Head for the ocean," commanded Jennifer. "As fast as you can, please."

Michael tried repeatedly to get an answer from Jerry's phone – but nothing.

Chapter fifty-five

Jeremy felt guilty about leaving Jennifer and Michael as he turned on to Sunset Boulevard. But he could not resist the thought of seeing Barbara again, however swiftly.

He reached into the phone booth, lifted the hand-set and dialled the Marriott. "Hello ?" Barbara's voice was soft and sleepy…….

At that moment Jeremy felt a sharp prod in his left side: "What ?…….." was the last word he uttered as he faintly heard a voice saying: "Hey buddy, you got somethin' we want. Now hand it over – fast."

Without waiting for a response his assailant, one of two hooded and roughly dressed in jeans and sneakers, one white one black, thrust a savage blow into his chest. Jeremy didn't have time to realise that he had been stabbed through the heart. His blood spurted on to the sidewalk.

Moments later a large black people carrier with blacked-out windows pulled up alongside the phone booth and Jeremy's attackers lifted his now inert body into the back seats. The vehicle sped off.

Chapter fifty-six

As the car floated effortlessly towards the Pacific Highway, Jennifer ordered the driver to head South to the airport.

Within minutes they pulled up at the British Airways check-in area. Jennifer stuffed a wad of notes in the driver's hand as Michael unpacked the bags onto a bell-boy's trolley.

Within the hour both Jennifer and Michael settled back into first-class seats. Jennifer had up-graded all three of them to minimise the delays at check-in.

"God, I do hope Jerry is OK, " said Jennifer," but I just knew we had to get out of there fast. Clancy is a very powerful man in the States and he can achieve almost anything."

"Including turning this plane back ?" mused Michael.

"No, I don't think he would do that. It might prove embarrassing for him to have to explain why he should do such a thing."

At that moment a cabin steward touched Jennifer lightly on the forearm. "Telephone call for you Mrs Hawes."

Shocked, Jennifer took the handset.

"Hi, Pammy. Why did you run out on me ?" said Clancy lightly.

"I – I have to get back to London and this is the only immediate flight. I didn't have time to tell you. I'm sorry. How did you find me ? I've actually changed my name since we last met."

"It helps to be Attorney-General of the United States as I told you before," said Clancy, his tone darkening. "Pammy, I have some bad news for you, I'm afraid. Your boy Jeremy is dead."

Jennifer gasped and dropped the phone, staring wildly ahead. Michael sensed a problem and picked up the phone. "This is Michael Leake, who is speaking?"

"Michael, it's Clancy Turner. I'm afraid I just had to tell your mother – she is _your_ mother, or is it Jeremy ?– that Jeremy is dead. He took some things from my room when you left, but it seems that some crack-head hustled him at a phone-box on Sunset Boulevard and he resisted just a little too much. I'm sorry to have to break the news."

"How do _you_ know so fast?" said Michael, still calm amidst the huge shock.

"I keep telling your mother that I am the Attorney General of the United States and I am supposed to know about crime, among other things." lied Clancy. "Can your mother speak now ?"

Jennifer nodded. She was deep in shock but still relatively calm. "I'm sorry, Pammy," continued the deep, dark voice of Clancy Turner, " but Sunset Boulevard can be a dangerous place at night. It doesn't pay to walk about in Hollywood.

"Now you all gonna have to come back to California real soon to help this investigation of the LAPD. "

"Of course we will," said a distraught Jennifer, not meaning a word of it.

"By the way, Jeremy took a coupla things from my room when he left. They weren't on him when the boys, that is the police, found him. Do you have any idea about that ?"

"I don't know what you're talking about,'" said Jennifer severely. "Now I am too upset to talk any more. Goodbye, Clancy." She clicked the 'off' button and motioned the steward to take the phone away. Then the tears started to fall and the great, heaving sobs took over her body as she burrowed down into Michael's arms for the rest of the flight.

Chapter fifty-seven

Jennifer had only recovered a little of her customary poise as she walked through the immigration area at Heathrow more than ten hours later. The immigration officer glanced at her passport and turned and nodded to two men standing some distance behind the line of desks.

They stepped forward briskly and introduced themselves. "Miss Hawes and, er, Mr Leake, I'm Detective-Superintendent Wilson and this is Sergeant Burrows. We're from the Metropolitan Police and we'd like to have a word with you in private if we may."

"Am I under arrest or something ?" said Jennifer irritated and exhausted after the long flight.

They moved to a small, sparsely-furnished office which earned its description by virtue of a small wooden desk and two plastic chairs. The policemen graciously allowed Jennifer and Michael to take the seats.

"I understand that you experienced a bereavement in Los Angeles, Ms Hawes and Mr Leake. Please accept our deepest sympathy.

"However, the authorities in Los Angeles, that is the Police Department there, have asked us to detain you as material witnesses to the death of Mr Jeremy Speake – would that be your brother, sir ?" asked the police officer rather unnecessarily.

"Yes," said Michael brusquely. " Look,. What is all this about ? My mother is deeply shocked and we just want to go home. We have already told the Attorney-General of the United States that we will return to assist the investigation in due course. Why should you detain us ? What grounds do you have for that ?"

"Well, none actually, sir. The LAPD boys don't quite understand our legal system here. They thought we could just put you back on the plane and Bob's your uncle, so to speak."

"Well ?" said Michael defiantly. "What now ? We want to go home and grieve for my brother. It's awful, the whole bloody thing."

"I wouldn't recommend that, actually sir. There's a huge posse of press boys outside in the arrivals hall and many more at your home, I shouldn't be at all surprised," said DS Wilson. "We simply want you to keep in touch with us and let us know your whereabouts during the next few days while the Yanks get their act together. Is there somewhere you could go that will be quieter than home ? I'm quite happy to escort you anywhere in London."

Michael was becoming extremely irritated by the avuncular manner of the police. But there was no disguising their authority and firm intent.

"What shall we do, mother ?"

"Can you get us away from here, superintendent ?" said Jennifer quietly. "I've had enough for one 24 hours."

"Yes, of course, madam. We can take you through a side exit to our car and no-one will be any the wiser. " He smiled at this apparent progress.

"OK, then take us to the Dorchester, please. We can hide there for a while," offered Jennifer, close now to collapse.

Chapter fifty-eight

'London Hostess in LA Murder Riddle' screamed the Evening Standard billboards when, much later in the day, Michael awoke and took a short stroll across the road into Hyde Park. He checked his mobile phone and found 47 messages recorded. He discarded all of them and started at what he felt was the beginning of being back in London after the death of his brother.

He wondered if it had all been worth the effort. Finding his mother certainly had been worth it, but this quest to identify his father had turned horribly wrong and Jeremy was now dead because of it.

He wrestled with the thought of whether to go through with identifying his father. How would he feel if his father was also dead ? How did he feel about the two candidates still alive ? He was not much impressed with Isaac Kernow as a man and had little wish to be connected with a disgraced politician – twice over.

Clancy Turner was an impressive but rather daunting figure. He had moved on somehow from reality and normality to that kind of uber-existence of the extremely powerful, the extremely rich and the extremely famous – sort of untouchable in many ways.

What would it be like to be a son of his, Michael wondered. Would he even admit to being his father. He was powerful enough to get away with almost anything, denying fatherhood would be relatively easy, although it might count against him were he eventually to become a Presidential candidate.

Maybe he was actually heir to Winscombe Hall. That would be quite something, but in a way it would be stealing from Jamie Avonborough's legitimate children and they had enough to deal with after their father's suicide.

Michael was then debating within himself the prospect of owning an ostentatious villa in the South of France and a share of an advertising man's fortune. Somehow he had already discounted the prospect of Eden James being his father. At their meeting he could not feel the slightest affinity for the man. There was no pooling of genes there, he felt sure.

Suddenly Michael stopped in his tracks. He had not been in touch with his actual father, who must be suffering badly with Jeremy's death. He quickly rang Jennifer to let her know where he was. He woke her up but she was pleased to speak to him and agreed that they should contact Sam Leake at once.

Michael strode back to the hotel and slipped in the side entrance. Already he was getting used to being some sort of fugitive.

Sam was in sombre mood and his wife Lucy was sedated and in bed. No matter how much they loved Michael, Jerry had been their flesh and their only natural child. They were devastated.

Nevertheless Sam immediately made arrangements for Jennifer and Michael to be collected in a blacked-out people carrier from the side door of the Dorchester and brought to his house in Surrey. He had developed a fine, five-bedroomed detached house with triple garage on the outskirts of Horley and virtually within sight of the runway at Gatwick Airport – handy for his many foreign excursions.

Rarely did the aircraft noise impinge upon the tranquillity of the Leake household thanks to careful research of the landing and taking-off patterns before the land was bought and the house built.

Sam and Michael, then Sam and Jennifer and Michael and Lucy hugged each other in turn as their mutual grief took over the house for the evening.

By morning, however, Sam had started to put plans into place. Jennifer had long since retrieved the tissues and small sliver of bloodstained glass from her bra and Sam sent it off in the hands of a trusted employee from his practice to the test laboratory where the three other tests had taken place and the results retained by the laboratory in a safe.

No formal results could be expected for several days. Jeremy's body was apparently being retained by the LAPD for forensic tests so the family could not begin to prepare for his funeral. These were to be the most testing days for everyone.

Three days later the tension broke. Superintendent Wilson and his faithful Sergeant Mullins arrived in Horley at Sam Leake's house, accompanied by an officer of the Surrey police just for good order.

"The Attorney-General's office in the United States has sent over an extradition request for Mrs Jennifer Hawes and Mr Michael Leake as material witnesses and possibly participants in the death of Mr Jeremy Leake in Los Angeles five days ago."

"What evidence do they have of any involvement of either Mrs Hawes or my son in Jerry's death?" demanded Sam Leake.

"As I'm sure you understand, sir, they are not obliged to offer any evidence but simply to state their belief that a crime has been committed and that these people have some intimate knowledge of it. I would like Mrs Hawes and Mr Leake, please, to accompany me to Paddington Green police station for service and acknowledgement of the extradition papers."

"Christ, man, they're still in shock over Jerry's death and clearly they had nothing to do with it," raged Sam. "We will appeal this request to every court in the land and probably Europe too. You can't just do this."

"I'm afraid I have no choice, sir. We must go to Paddington Green. It may be that there will be a few more days yet before arrangements can be made to transport Mrs Hawes and Mr Leake back to Los Angeles, in which case they may return here to your custody Mr Leake until further advised.

"Then they will have to report to Heathrow at a designated time and law officers from the United States will meet them on board a plane for Los Angeles and take them into custody on arrival."

"This is outrageous," fumed Sam. He turned to Jennifer and Michael and said quietly and out of earshot of the policemen, who stood off rather embarrassed at their role of stooges for the United States legal system.

"Look, you have to go with them, but my office is already working on strategies to get this request annulled. I am sure something can be worked out. Keep in touch with your phones. I'm hoping to get the test results later today so that might give us something."

"OK, dad," said Michael. "I've filed my piece on Clancy Turner, so I hope it doesn't spoil the process."

"I'm sure the Chronicle's lawyers are crawling all over it. But the paper will want to get it out while you two are such a hot property , as it were."

Jennifer remained deeply in shock, not really caring what was happening to her. Her new-found love had been wrenched from her as suddenly as her last and the pain was no less intense.

She and Michael climbed into the back of the marked police car with a second acting as escort and the two sped off towards London.

They ducked as the cars drove at some speed into the yard at London's high security police station at Paddington Green because the media had already been tipped off and was camped out hoping to get a glimpse of the Socialite and her New Found Son – this one was going to run and run.

Inside the station the couple were treated with courtesy and some consideration, which at least stretched to the occasional cup of tea. Eventually a sergeant arrived with a small sheaf of papers, which appeared to be the official request for their extradition to Los Angeles.

Just then Jennifer's phone rang. It was Sam. He had the results of all four DNA tests and there was one certain result, which he was about to act upon immediately.

Jennifer smiled as the tension drained from her face. She passed the phone to the sergeant who had been droning on about the ins and outs of the extradition treaty between the United Kingdom and the United States. She whispered to Michael: "It's over. We know who your father is."

"I see, I see," the sergeant kept repeating as he listened to Sam Leake. "Well of course, we will have to get confirmation from America before we can let them go, sir and that could take a few hours."

He turned to Jennifer and Michael after giving her the phone back and said: "It seems there has been a development which might make all this unnecessary. But as I say, we need to get confirmation from the United States before you can leave, I'm afraid. Mr Leake says he is on his way here."

And a few hours it was before Sam Leake led Jennifer and Michael out into the bright late afternoon sunshine to face a battery of cameras, reporters and television crews close to the Edgeware Road fly-over.

He laughed and pointed their attention to a newspaper billboard on the far side of Edgeware Road outside the tube station. It read simply:

'US Attorney General Resigns.'

Printed in Great Britain
by Amazon